THE HAUNTING OF FREDDY

BOOK FOUR

IN THE GOLDEN
HAMSTER SAGA

BY Dietlof Reiche

TRANSLATED FROM THE GERMAN BY John Brownjohn

ILLUSTRATED BY Joe Cepeda

SCHOLASTIC INC.
NEW YORK TORONTO LONDON AUCKLAND SYDNEY
MEXICO CITY NEW DELHI HONG KONG BUENOS AIRES

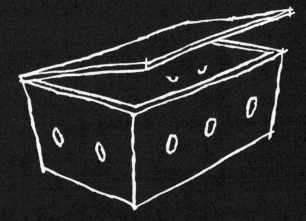

Text copyright © 2001 by Beltz Verlag, Weinheim und Basel

Programm Anrich, Weinheim

Illustrations copyright © 2006 by Joe Cepeda

Translation copyright © 2006 by Scholastic Inc.

Published by Scholastic Inc., by arrangement with Beltz Verlag, Weinheim und Basel.

SCHOLASTIC and associated logos are trademarks

and/or registered trademarks of Scholastic Inc.

ISBN-13: 978-0-439-53160-3

ISBN-10: 0-439-53160-8

12 11 10 9 8 7 6 5 4 3 2 1   7 8 9 10 11/0

Printed in the U.S.A.   23

First trade paperback printing, March 2007

Text type set in 14-point Perpetua

Display type set in Johnny Lunchpail

Book design by Marijka Kostiw

Chapter One

The rabbits were quite unsuspecting.

They were sound asleep in their warren, and nowhere, not even in the innermost recesses of their usually timid and wary souls, did they harbor the slightest suspicion that certain preparations were in progress outside — preparations designed to ensure that all of them (they numbered more than a dozen) would be dead by noon.

It was an oppressively hot and humid day in the summer of 1593, and the sultry weather may have been to blame for their lack of vigilance. They had posted no lookouts, so the tall, dark, grim-faced man was able to go about his sinister business unobserved.

He began by draping nets over five of the six rabbit holes and securing them by means of foot-long iron stakes, which he quietly embedded in the ground. Then he laid a wooden club on the ground, ready just in case (the rabbits that got caught in his nets were generally "dispatched," as he put it, by a blow with the back of his hand). Finally, he deposited a wooden box beside the one rabbit hole that had no net over it.

This box displayed careful workmanship despite its rough exterior, and air holes had been neatly drilled in its sides at regular intervals. The tall, grim-faced man unfastened the lid and folded it back, then reached inside with both hands. When he withdrew them, each

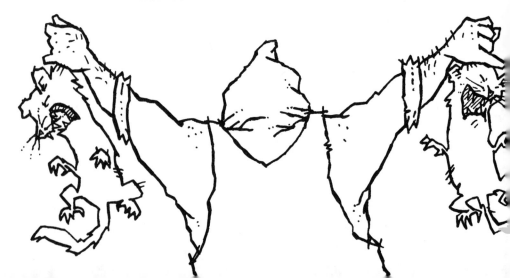

was holding a ferret. The ferrets were exceptionally large — almost as long as a man's arm — and had thick, yellowish fur. They opened their mouths so wide, one could see past their needle-sharp teeth and down their throats. And issuing from those throats came . . .

. . . a snarl!

I'd heard **a SNaRL.**

It was such a piercing, vicious sound that my mental command center issued a **RED aLERT.** I sprang to my feet and reared up on my haunches. My fur stood on end as if someone had brushed it the wrong way.

It was the kind of loud, ferocious snarl made by ferrets when hunting. Any moment now, they would invade the warren and race along the underground tunnels, spreading panic and terror in their wake, and then . . . The snarl died away.

Besides, there wasn't any rabbit warren here.

I slowly sat down again.

This was Mr. John's apartment — his home and ours (mine and the other animals', I mean).

I was seated on the desk at the computer keyboard, and on the screen in front of me were the words I'd just written. They were the opening words of my latest story, "The Lord of the Ferrets."

Well, what do you know! I'd been so spellbound by what I'd typed with my own two paws, I'd actually heard the imaginary ferrets hiss. Not bad, Mr. Author! That's what they call truly realistic writing.

It was just after midnight, a time when we golden hamsters are wider awake than most humans are during the day. Mr. John is asleep at this hour — fortunately, because it enables me to use the computer undisturbed. No one interrupts me, neither Sir William, the civilized tomcat (with whom I get on pretty well — as long as I abide by his rules), nor Enrico and Caruso, the singing guinea pigs, who have become quite celebrated thanks to my literary activities. Need I say more about those two buffoons?

All right: They're the most slovenly, impudent guinea pigs I know. How many guinea pigs *do* I know? Only those two, but — to be absolutely frank — they're two too many. Believe it or not, Enrico and Caruso don't have a smidgen of respect for me — *me*, the only golden hamster famed throughout the world for his ability to read and write! **OKAY, FREDDY, COOL IT.**

In any event, it's a mercy that guinea pigs are active during the day. In other words, at night, when my kind get down to some serious work, those two clowns are fast asleep in their cage (which Mr. John, for some unaccountable reason, always leaves open).

Sir William isn't exactly a fan of my book-writing either, I might add. This afternoon, when I told him about my new story, he listened benevolently at first. But then, sounding genuinely concerned, he said, "Freddy, my friend, are you sure it doesn't overtax your brain, thinking up these stories? You're a golden hamster, after all, and nature designed your brain for other purposes." In other words, Sir William thinks it's abnormal for a

5

golden hamster to write books. Never mind, I know what's good for me.

I reread what I'd written on the screen. Yes, it was pretty good. Carry on, Freddy.

> The ferrets were exceptionally large — almost as long as a man's arm — and had thick, yellowish fur. They opened their mouths so wide, one could see past their needle-sharp teeth and down their throats. And issuing from those throats came a snarl. It was such a piercing, ferocious snarl that . . .

I sprang to my feet again.

Some ferrets were definitely snarling, and the sound came from somewhere in this room. But . . . no, I wasn't imagining things — I could really hear them! I could even locate the sound. It was coming from just below me.

I dashed over to the miniature rope ladder suspended from the opposite side of the desk and climbed down it in silence. Although it was darker on the floor than on the desk, I could see pretty well in the reflected glow from the screen.

I SPOTTED THE PAiR OF THEM aT ONCE.

They were hunkered down precisely where my ears had located them, and they had their backs to me. I stole closer. And then, just as I came up behind them, they stopped snarling. That's great, you guys — perfect positioning!

I drew a deep breath and darted past them. Then, spinning around, I rose on my haunches, inflated my cheek pouches, and emitted a snarl as piercing and ferocious as that of any ferret.

Enrico and Caruso fell over.

WHOOPS! Each of them fell flat on his back with all four legs in the air. They do this every time. A guinea pig's alarm system isn't designed to cope with the sight of a hamster in fighting mode, simply because nature hasn't allowed for such a contingency. The result is, Enrico and Caruso get such a terrible shock, it knocks them flat.

Enrico is small and skinny, with long red-and-white fur. Caruso, by contrast, is big and fat and has a short black-and-white coat. Grunting and groaning, they scrambled to their feet.

"You know what that was for?" I demanded.

They nodded. "Did we give you a terrible fright?" asked Enrico, looking genuinely contrite and remorseful — or so I thought.

"Yes," I said — stupidly.

"It worked, Caruso!" Enrico cried delightedly, and Caruso chortled, "That'll teach him!"

Whereupon they chanted in unison:

"Two friendly guinea pigs are we.
No animals could nicer be,
and yet, however hard we labor
to entertain our grouchy neighbor,
he makes a rotten audience
because he always takes offense."

I gasped. Grouchy neighbor? Friendly guinea pigs? They'd turned the truth on its head! Who was always tormenting whom? I trembled with rage. So one knockdown wasn't enough for you, I thought. Just you wait! I reared up on my haunches again.

"Freddy, my friend," I heard, "do I have to remind you that we're all one family here, and that 'Fair play' is our family's Rule No. 1?" Sir William was standing right behind me.

Sir William, who's the biggest, blackest tomcat

imaginable, is equipped with a set of most impressive fangs. What's more, he considers it unfair of me to flatten Enrico and Caruso by adopting my hostile hamster pose.

What this boils down to is, when Sir William disapproves of something, it's wiser not to do it. I sat down again.

He turned to Enrico and Caruso. "Congratulations, boys. Those snarls of yours sounded thoroughly realistic." Having at some stage appointed the pair of them his court jesters, Sir William always makes favorable comments on their performances. They bowed like actors taking a curtain call.

"However," Sir William went on, "I must also reprimand you. Your snarls were so loud, they might have woken Mr. John. **SHAME ON YOU!**" He eyed them sternly, whereupon they hung their heads and gave an imitation of two conscience-stricken guinea pigs. "The same goes for you, of course," he added, turning to

10

me. I too hung my head for safety's sake, even though I found his concern for Mr. John's slumbers a trifle exaggerated.

He did have a point, though. Mr. John slept in the next room with the door ajar, so he might well have heard us snarling. He couldn't have heard what we said, however, because we were communicating in Interanimal, the telepathic language used by all mammals except humans.

"In the future," said Sir William, "kindly observe Rule No. 2: MR. JOHN'S SLEEP IS SACRED." To call his concern a trifle exaggerated was a gross understatement. "And now," he went on, "I bid the diurnally active members of our family good night and wish the nocturnally active member a successful night's work." He pricked up his ears suddenly. There were sounds of movement in the room next door.

A moment later the light came on, the door opened, and Mr. John appeared.

Mr. John is very tall, with a big nose and bushy eyebrows. He's a fine figure of a man, but the floral pajamas he was wearing didn't exactly show him off to his best advantage.

"Hello, kids." He nodded to us. "Everything okay? I thought I heard a noise."

I ran to my rope ladder, climbed onto the desk, and darted over to the keyboard. *Everything's fine, Mr. John,* I typed. It's one of our rules that Mr. John must never be burdened with any disputes that arise between us animals. This rule (Rule No. 3, if I've counted correctly) was laid down by me, not — for a change — by Sir William. It means, among other things, that I make sure Mr. John is spared all knowledge of the guinea pigs' boorish behavior.

Sorry, Mr. John, I typed. *I guess I must have hit the keys too hard.*

Mr. John yawned. "That's okay. Good night, kids."

Just as he turned to go, something occurred to me. *Could you get the book out for me?* I typed quickly.

He understood right away. "The judgments?" he asked, and I nodded. He went over to the bookshelf, removed the book, and put it down beside the keyboard.

Thanks, I typed.

"You're welcome, kid," he said, and disappeared into his bedroom followed by Sir William, who sleeps on a blanket in there. Enrico and Caruso toddled off to their cage.

I was alone once more. Alone with my story.

AND THE BOOK.

It was an old book published in the eighteenth century. The cover was missing and the pages were tattered. That was one reason why Mr. John had acquired it so cheaply, the other being that the bookseller thought it was deadly dull. Unlike him, Mr. John had recognized at once what a mine of information it could provide for an author like me.

"Here, kid," he'd said, "I think there's some stuff in there that may interest you."

I looked at the title and was promptly hooked:

The eighteenth-century editor had sifted through some old English court records and collected various judgments dating from times when the penalties imposed by law were harsh in the extreme. I had opened the book at random and read:

In one city of the realm, where the weaver's trade was flourishing, a master weaver named George Carver fashioned a copy of the seal of the Weavers' Guild and used this counterfeit for his own illicit purposes. On Friday, the 14th day of May in the Year of Our Lord 1613, notwithstanding the fact that he had passed the age of 70, and as an example to other malefactors, he was sentenced to die by the ax.

So someone had forged a seal and been beheaded for it. If that wouldn't make a good story for an author, what would? But . . . had he forged the seal for personal profit, or had he been compelled to do so because he was starving? I would have had to opt for one of those two alternatives. Hmm . . . Being a hamster, on the other hand, I preferred to write a story featuring animals. Were there any such cases? I read on:

In a small barony in the West Country, a certain poacher was subjected to harsher punishment than anyone could remember. The said poacher, whom folk called Grim Harry on account of his sinister cast of feature, had killed three rabbits on the Baron's land with the aid of two ferrets. On the 30th day of August, Anno Domini 1593, having been apprehended and imprisoned, he was sentenced by the Baron, sitting in judgment, to die on the gallows as a dire example to others. The ferrets, which were exceptionally large, had previously, being guilty of the same offense as Grim Harry, been drowned without mercy.

THaT WaS iT! I had my case.

I had set about planning my next story, "The Lord of the Ferrets," the very same night.

If I'd had the slightest idea what a can of worms I was opening, I would have kept my paws to myself.

15

CHaPTER TWO

THEN A LETTER CAME for Mr. John.

That wasn't unusual in itself. Mr. John gets plenty of letters, but this one *was* unusual. It arrived the day before the night on which I started to write my story. The first thing I noticed after the mailman had pushed it through the slot in the front door (we live in a city where mail is delivered to the door, even when your home is on the top floor of an apartment house) was a scent of violets. The envelope smelled like a whole bunch of them. It was pale blue, an unusual shape (almost square), and bore a stamp I didn't recognize.

"Hmm," said Mr. John, eyeing it. "From England. That's odd. . . ." I had a good view of what he found odd. (Although it was long after breakfast and past my bedtime, I was sitting beside the computer because I like to watch him at work — even a superintelligent hamster never stops learning.) The address was written in dark blue ink in a spiky, almost illegible hand. Mr. John turned the envelope over. There was no sender's address on the back, but the thick paper was embossed with a coat of arms.

Mr. John slit open the envelope and removed the letter, which was also written in dark blue ink on pale blue paper. "Hmm," he said again. "It's from a Lady Templeton. Very odd indeed . . ." He proceeded to read the letter with many a "Hmm" and "Mmm," wrinkling his brow and shaking his head.

What on earth had the lady written? When Mr. John had finished reading the letter, he lowered it and sat there in silence, then proceeded to reread it from the beginning. **I COULDN'T ENDURE THE SUSPENSE ANY LONGER.**

Mr. John, I typed, and he looked up, *I don't mean*

to be indiscreet, but may I be permitted to know what's in the letter?

He nodded. "Certainly. It concerns you — and not you alone. First, though, I'm going to check." He reached for the telephone and dialed a number, which he read off the letterhead. I heard a faint ringing tone, followed by the sound of a voice.

"Lady Templeton?" said Mr. John. "I just received your letter. . . . That's right, I'm Mr. John. . . . Yes, I'm delighted too. . . . That's why I'm calling. Forgive me for asking, Your Ladyship, but did you really mean what you wrote? Hmm . . . No, not yet, but I'll get down to it right away. . . . Yes, of course, I'll let you know as soon as possible. . . . Good-bye." Mr. John replaced the receiver, plucking thoughtfully at his left eyebrow.

Suddenly, he called, "**KIDS!** We've got something to discuss!"

This was the signal for what Sir William refers to as a family council. I'd prefer to call it a conference attended

not only by
rational beings but
also, unfortunately, by two
scatterbrained guinea pigs.

We hold these conferences on
the desk. (Mr. John naturally sits beside it on
his swivel chair, because what we animals say can
be communicated to him only by me via the
computer screen.) Sir William, with one mighty
leap, jumped up there by himself; Enrico and
Caruso, who are about as good at jumping as sacks
of potatoes, had to be lifted onto the desk
by Mr. John, but not before he'd
draped an old rug over it. (Look in any
encyclopedia, and you won't find guinea pigs
mentioned under the headword *Housebroken*.)

"Kids," Mr. John began, "this letter is addressed to us
all. 'Dear Mr. John,'" he read aloud, "'dear Freddy, dear
Sir William, dear Enrico and Caruso . . .'"

19

WHaT? No special form of address for me? "Dear Freddy" put me on the same level as those guinea pigs. Lady Templeton obviously didn't appreciate my uniqueness.

Sir William was clearly flattered to be addressed by his title. "Freddy, my friend," he said, "please would you ask Mr. John the identity of this person who expresses him or herself in such a well-bred manner?"

Mr. John, I wrote on the screen, *Sir William is consumed with curiosity. He wants to know the person's name and what they say in their letter.* (Sir William can't read, so I phrase his questions rather loosely.)

Mr. John grinned. "The name of the woman — or rather, the lady — is Agatha, Baroness Templeton."

Sir William merely nodded, as if a letter addressed to him, among others, could only have been written by a member of the aristocracy.

"As for the contents of the letter," Mr. John went on, looking at it, "— well, I'll read you the crucial sentence."

The sentence Mr. John proceeded to read aloud was crucial indeed. It heralded a chain of events that proved hair-raising in the literal sense, at least where we animals were concerned. As for the humans involved . . . But no, first things first.

" 'And now,' " Mr. John read aloud, " 'I should like to ask whether you and the animals would consent to be my guests for a while, here at Templeton Castle.' " He lowered the letter and looked at each of us in turn.

An invitation to stay at this woman's castle? Hmm. Why should she invite us at all? That question would have to be resolved before we decided whether to accept.

Sir William had curled his tail elegantly around him. "In my opinion," he purred, "to be invited to stay at a baronial castle is a great honor."

Typical of him. A baroness had only to crook her little finger and His Lordship came running. It would never occur to him to wonder what might lie behind the invitation.

"But before we accept," Sir William went on, "we must ascertain why Her Ladyship has invited us at all."

I ought to have felt ashamed of myself, I guess, but I'd forgotten how to.

"Freddy, my dear fellow, would you be good enough to put that question to Mr. John?"

I did so, and Mr. John consulted the letter again. "Well," he said at length, "she cites only one reason for the invitation. She writes: 'I'm an ardent admirer of the great literary skill so impressively displayed by the author of the Freddy books.' Those are her actual words."

So the woman obviously *did* appreciate my uniqueness!

"Well," said Mr. John, "it all sounds very nice, but there's something I find a little worrying."

WORRYING? What could be worrying about an ardent admirer of mine? *What's that, Mr. John?* I typed.

"Well, putting two and two together — the letter, the handwriting, the phraseology, and, most of all, the voice on the phone . . ." Mr. John cleared his throat. "I can't help coming to the following conclusion: She must be as old as Methuselah."

I saw Enrico and Caruso exchange a glance.

So what? I typed defiantly. *Old folk like the Freddy books too.*

"Sure, kid." Mr. John nodded. "Except that I wonder if the old lady has gathered who actually writes them."

At that precise moment, after sitting meekly on their blanket for a suspiciously long time, Enrico and Caruso launched into one of their performances.

"I beg Your Ladyship's pardon," said Caruso, impersonating a dignified butler, "but your visitor is here."

"Is that so, James? Excellent, excellent." Enrico had slipped into the role of a wizened old baroness. "The author of the celebrated Freddy books? Excellent. Show him in, James."

"Pardon me, Your Ladyship, but I already did."

"Is that so?" The baroness looked around. "But where is he? I can't see anyone."

"Here, Your Ladyship." Caruso extended his right forepaw. "Here on my hand."

"On your, er, hand?" The baroness pretended to hold a lorgnette to her eyes and stared at Caruso's paw, then uttered a sudden, shrill scream. **EEEK!** It's a hamster, James! I'm allergic to hamster fur! How could you?!"

"Your Ladyship gave express orders that, when the author of the celebrated Freddy books arrived, I should —"

"GET RID OF THE BRUTE! AT ONCE!

Caruso pretended to toss something out the window. "No sooner said than done, Your Ladyship."

"Thank goodness for that." The baroness paused for a moment. Then she said, "Am I allergic to the fur of any other animals, James?"

"Not that I'm aware, Your Ladyship."

"Excellent. After a traumatic experience like that, I feel in need of a little cheering up. I propose to invite some really first-rate entertainers to the castle."

"And who might they be, Your Ladyship?"

"There are only two worth considering, James: Enrico and Caruso, the famous double act."

Whereupon the said double act flung their paws around each other and screeched with laughter.

At this point, I should like to state for the record how remarkable I find it that Enrico and Caruso manage to improvise their skits at the drop of a hat. Still more remarkable, not to say admirable, is the composure and self-restraint with which I always greet their attempts to pour scorn on my hamsterdom, my literary activities — indeed, my whole existence. Forget self-restraint! What they really deserved was a good bite in the backside from a hamster's razor-sharp teeth! Okay, I told myself, calm down.

Sir William, who had been watching me, nodded approvingly. As he saw it, I'd controlled myself well. It went without saying that he himself had found the skit an absolute hoot; in fact, I'd have bet three luscious mealworms on it.

"Boys," he told Enrico and Caruso, "that skit of yours was an absolute hoot." He turned to me. "No offense, my friend."

Of course not, Sir William. A bighearted hamster like me can take everything that's thrown at him.

"Kids," said Mr. John, "I think we ought to get on with our discussion."

"**GOOD HEAVENS!**" Sir William's eyes widened in consternation. "We've been keeping Mr. John waiting. How very embarrassing!"

You see, Sir William? That's what happens when you're a fan of two stupid guinea pigs.

"Freddy," he went on, "please, would you apologize to Mr. John on our —"

"Will do," I replied. I was already typing: *We apologize for the delay.*

Mr. John nodded. "No problem," he said. Then he typed, *Enrico and Caruso were obviously giving a performance just now. May I know what it was?*

They were doing a skit about a baroness and her butler. I hesitated. *The majority of us found it amusing.*

"Oh?" said Mr. John. He looked at me closely. *What about the minority?* he typed.

I hesitated again. I had no wish to break my own rule by dragging him into a dispute between us animals, but I felt justified in typing the following reply: *The minority of one thought their skit was rather silly.*

Mr. John eyed me a moment longer. Then he typed, *Okay, kid, forget I ever asked.* He paused before adding, *Well, what do you think? Should we accept the invitation?*

I debated the question. A vacation at an English castle? As an author, I could only benefit from a change of scene. On the other hand, Mr. John was probably right in surmising that the old baroness didn't realize the Freddy books were actually written by a golden hamster, so I wasn't particularly keen to meet her. Besides, I wanted to get on with my story.

Well, kid? Mr. John typed. *Yes or no?*

No, I typed back.

Mr. John thought a while. Then he said aloud, "Listen, you guys. I suggest we leave our decision to chance — make it dependent on whether or not Linda can find the time to drive us to the airport. Okay?"

Sir William and Enrico and Caruso nodded.

I was outvoted anyway, so I nodded likewise — hoping that Linda would be too busy.

CHapTER THREE

SHE WASN'T TOO BUSY.

Linda Carson is Mr. John's girlfriend. She owns a car, unlike Mr. John, who says he doesn't need one. Linda used to be a press reporter, but she now works for a local TV station. "I hardly ever use my laptop these days," she said. "You can take it with you, if you like."

This would enable us animals to communicate with Mr. John while we were away from his own computer. What was more, I could go on writing my story. That thought reconciled me a little to the prospect of Templeton Castle.

Besides, Mr. John couldn't get a cheap flight to England for another two weeks, so I might even be able to finish "The Lord of the Ferrets" before we left.

But it was strange: I couldn't get beyond the beginning. Ever since the letter arrived, I'd lost my ability to work on the story — why, I couldn't tell. I knew precisely how it ought to go and was eager to get cracking, but every time I tried to make a start,

SOME UNSEEN HAND SEEMED TO PIN DOWN MY PAWS.

"It's what they call writer's block," Mr. John told me. "Every genuine author gets it at least twice in his life." Although I felt flattered that he rated me a genuine author, his explanation didn't really satisfy me. What caused writer's block? Not even Mr. John could tell me that. "But a change of scene can sometimes work

wonders," he said. After that, I couldn't wait to get to Templeton Castle.

The day of our departure came at last. Linda — all lustrous red hair and apple-and-peach-blossom perfume — drove us to the airport in her car (one of those economical little buggies). Mr. John sat beside her in the passenger seat while Sir William, Enrico, Caruso, and I hunkered down on the shelf at the rear. Mr. John's suitcase had been put in the trunk with our traveling box, a special container with ventilation holes in the sides, like that of the ferrets in my story.

I shall refrain from giving my readers a detailed account of our flight to England. Suffice it to say that I dozed most of the way, lulled by the incessant drone of the engines. The rest of the time I devoted to literature. Not to "The Lord of the Ferrets" (I wouldn't go back to that till we got to Templeton Castle), but to a poem. I was still short of material for *A Hamster in Love*, the volume of poetry I'm planning to publish. This, I'm quite certain, will set entirely new standards in the field of golden-hamsterish verse.

I intended to write another poem for Sophie, who was my mistress before she sent me to live with Mr. John (because her mom was allergic to hamster fur). At present she was on vacation with her parents. I wanted to e-mail her the poem from Templeton Castle (she doesn't possess a computer herself, but Gregory, her father, does) so as to give her a treat as soon as she came home.

It was hard work, especially as there wasn't enough room in our traveling box for Linda's laptop, but I had the verses stored in my head:

TO SOPHIE
The very thought of you, my dear,
is one I cherish very much.
My eyes light up when you are near,
my whiskers quiver at your touch.
Cheek pouches swelling with delight,
I fill my nostrils with your scent.
Whene'er my eyes on you alight,
no hamster could feel more content.

I doubt if many girls receive poems of such quality from a golden hamster.

Templeton Castle wasn't a castle at all.
    I'd been expecting to see a magnificent old building topped with battlements and enclosed by a moat.

What confronted us looked more like a farmhouse
surrounded by plowed fields and a few clumps of trees.

There was a stone gateway, however, and when
our taxi drove through it into the courtyard, the main
building made a more massive impression than it

had from a distance. There was even a tower at one end, not particularly high but sturdily constructed and overgrown with ivy from ground to roof. Templeton Castle might have been a castle once upon a time, but all that remained of it was a kind of oversized manor house.

It was quite a big property, counting the main house and its two annexes. A bit too big for the Templeton family's bank account, perhaps, because the walls were crumbling and some of the roof tiles were missing.

The taxi turned and drove off, leaving Mr. John standing there with his suitcase and our traveling box. It was four o'clock, and the courtyard lay empty and deserted in the afternoon sun. **NOTHING STIRRED** No sign of life anywhere.

"Hmm," said Mr. John. "They must have heard us. I told the old lady we'd be here at four. Mind you, it's two weeks since we spoke on the phone. It may have slipped her memory. Let's hope she hasn't forgotten our visit altogether."

At that moment the front door opened and a man emerged. He stared in our direction, shielding his eyes from the sun with one hand, then walked across the courtyard toward us.

He was wearing an old tweed jacket with leather elbow patches, dirty brown corduroy pants, and a pair of even dirtier gumboots (an English expression, I learned later). "Yes?" he said, eyeing Mr. John with a frown. He didn't look downright hostile, just suspicious.

"Good afternoon," Mr. John said politely. "Would you be kind enough to inform Lady Templeton of our arrival?"

"What are you talking about?" That *did* sound hostile.

Mr. John remained polite. "Please inform Her Ladyship that her visitors are here."

"VISITORS? I know nothing of any visitors."

"Could it be," said Mr. John, controlling himself with an effort, "that Her Ladyship may have invited us without consulting you first?"

"I doubt it." The man stared at Mr. John in silence.

Then he said, "I own this place, you see. I'm Lord Templeton."

"Oh," said Mr. John, but the speed with which he recovered his composure was admirable. He introduced himself as if conversing with stubble-chinned English aristocrats in grubby old jackets and corduroy pants were a daily habit of his. (He neglected to introduce us animals, but I didn't resent that in light of the awkwardness of the situation.)

"I'm sorry," Mr. John said, "but it appears that Her Ladyship, er . . ."

"My aunt," said Lord Templeton. "My aunt Agatha."

". . . it appears that your aunt invited us without informing you." Mr. John produced the old lady's letter from his breast pocket and held it out. "Just to show you that I'm not suffering from delusions."

Lord Templeton examined the letter. "Yes, that's definitely her handwriting." He handed it back. "Aunt Agatha's recent behavior was a little — how shall I put it? —ECCENTRIC."

Her recent behavior *was* . . . I didn't think twice about his use of the past tense, I admit, but neither did Mr. John. "Eccentric?" he said. "Oh, I understand."

"*I* don't," Sir William whispered to me.

I tapped my forehead with my paw, and he nodded.

Mr. John squared his shoulders. "Our invitation was obviously based on a misunderstanding," he said, very politely. "I naturally consider the matter closed. We'll leave at once."

That really got Lord Templeton's goat. "HOW DARE YOU!" he said, glaring at Mr. John. "You were invited and you're staying — you and that menagerie of yours!" Mr. John started to say something, but Lord Templeton cut him short. "If you leave now, I shall take it as a personal insult, is that clear?!"

Mr. John nodded mutely.

Lord Templeton turned to go. "I'll inform the housekeeper. She'll help you to settle in." And he stomped off.

Suddenly, however, he came to a halt and turned back, but he didn't look at us, just stared at the ground for a while. At last he said, "I suppose I'd better tell you." He looked up. "AUNT AGATHA DIED TWO WEEKS AGO."

40

Chapter Four

MY PAWS HAD TWITCHED.

They'd twitched as if I were typing.

It happened just as Lord Templeton said "Aunt Agatha died two weeks ago." The sensation was only momentary but quite unmistakable.

He crossed the courtyard and disappeared into the house. Mr. John stood staring after him, then turned to us. "I wonder if we should stay, under the circumstances," he said. "Probably not." He looked back at the house.

How on earth could I get at Linda's laptop? I simply had to persuade him to stay. "Sir William," I began, but Mr. John was speaking again.

"No, we can't," he said firmly, "even if His Lordship *does* take offense. I'll ask them to call for a taxi, and we'll —" He broke off. A girl had emerged from the front door. She came dashing across the courtyard, auburn hair flying.

"Hello," she said breathlessly, "I'm Annabelle."

Annabelle was around twelve years old. She beamed at Mr. John. "I thought Daddy was pulling my leg at first, but he wasn't." Her smile broadened. "You're here, just fancy! I've got all the Freddy books. Where is he?" Like Sir William and Enrico and Caruso, I was sitting on the ground at Mr. John's feet. She caught sight of me at last. "Oh, there you are! How do you do, Freddy?"

Annabelle not only had auburn hair, she had a sprinkling of funny little freckles. She also smelled so sweetly of fresh chamomile blossom, my nose was positively captivated.

I sat up on my haunches, and then — no, I didn't go straight into my routine: I performed it slowly and deliberately, as if for the very first time. I sat up and begged, made myself as tall as I could, and finally . . . I waved.

42

"HE'S WAVING!" Annabelle exclaimed delightedly. "So you really *can* wave, Freddy! I thought it was just a story." She turned to Mr. John. "You mean it's all true, what it says in the Freddy books?"

"As Freddy might say," said Mr. John, "yes, paw on heart."

Annabelle laughed. Suddenly, though, she turned serious. "Daddy says Great-Aunt Agatha invited you. I wonder why she never told us?"

"Perhaps she meant to, but then she . . ."

". . . died. Yes, maybe." Annabelle pointed to one of the annexes. "That's where she lived, all by herself. Had her own telephone, et cetera. We didn't see much of her. Bertha — that's our housekeeper — was the only one who got on with her. She was a little bit . . . well, peculiar sometimes." She paused. "A few days before she died she came and borrowed all my Freddy books."

"Hmm," said Mr. John. "Was it really so peculiar for an elderly lady to want to read the Freddy books?"

"Of course not." Annabelle shook her head. "The

peculiar thing was: **HOW DID SHE KNOW I HAD THE BOOKS?** I never mentioned them to her, and I'm sure the others didn't either." She looked over at the larger of the two annexes. "Bertha found her. She said she looked as if she'd been scared to death by some frightful apparition."

The silence that followed was broken by a sudden shout.

"Hey, Annabelle, I'd like a honey sandwich!"

A plump little boy was standing in the doorway. He had the same auburn hair as Annabelle but looked younger.

"Make it yourself!" Annabelle called back. "That's my brother, Sebastian," she told Mr. John. "He expects me to do everything for him, now that Mummy's not here."

Sebastian walked across the courtyard toward us. He really was quite fat. "You're mean," he said to Annabelle, then turned to Mr. John. "So you're the man in the Freddy books. Just so you know, I don't read storybooks.

I think storybooks are silly, especially ones with animals in them."

"I'm sorry," said Mr. John, "— sorry for your sake."

Sebastian just grinned. He looked down at us and said, "Hey, you've got a regular zoo here."

Annabelle indicated me. "That's Freddy."

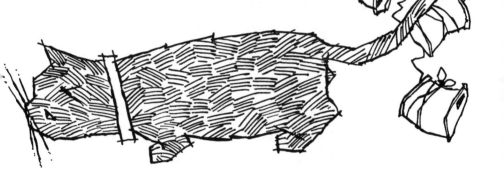

I politely sat up and begged, but Sebastian ignored me. He eyed Sir William as if planning to tie an empty can to his tail in the very near future. Then he pointed to Enrico and Caruso and started laughing. He bent down and made a grab for them, but they eluded him. "Hey, come here, you funny little things!"

"LEAVE THEM ALONE!" Annabelle snapped, sounding really angry. "They aren't things, they're Enrico and Caruso." Looking down at us, she said, "You animals must be very careful when you go outdoors. There are lots of buzzards hereabouts." She glared at Sebastian. "And don't go playing any of your silly tricks on them either."

Sebastian grinned. "I don't know what you mean." He straightened up. "Anyway, this is boring." And he ambled off across the courtyard without another word.

Annabelle stared after him and sighed. "He thinks it's cool to act that way." She looked up at the sky. "Oh dear, there's a storm brewing." Dark clouds were gathering in the distance and the wind was rising. "You must come inside. I'll go and ask Bertha what rooms you can have." She ran back to the house and disappeared.

Mr. John plucked at one of his bushy eyebrows. "All things considered, I guess we'd better stay."

Annabelle reemerged from the house, followed by a woman in an apron — a tall woman with muscular arms. **"HELLO,"** she said in a voice as deep as a man's, "I'm

Bertha." Mr. John started to say something, but she went on: "I know, you're the American with the animals. I'll have a word with you about *them* later. First we must see where to put you and your zoo." She jerked her thumb at the main house. "The fact is, it's not so easy to find anywhere habitable in the old place."

Bertha eventually assigned us two rooms in the tower. Situated one above the other and connected by a staircase, they were not only spacious but light, the arrow slits having at some point been widened to form windows. Mr. John moved into the upper room, we animals into the lower. Bertha had even managed to dig out some old cages for me and the guinea pigs.

"Right," she said to Mr. John (Annabelle had reluctantly gone off for a piano lesson), "about these animals of yours. They're weird and wonderful creatures, so Annabelle says. That's why I'm prepared to let them roam around free — for the time being. But I'll tell you one thing. . . ." She leveled her finger at Enrico and Caruso. "If those two pee in the wrong place, even once, outside they go. It'll be into the stable with them, is that clear?"

"As daylight," said Mr. John. "You don't mince your words, do you?"

Bertha snorted. "I believe in speaking my mind."

"I meant it as a compliment," Mr. John said with a smile.

"I've heard nicer ones," growled Bertha. She put her hands on her hips. "Anyway, anyone who makes a mess is out." She walked to the door, then turned and pointed at me. "**THIS HaMSTER—** can he really read and write?"

"Yes," said Mr. John.

"And he actually writes whole books?"

"He certainly does."

She shook her head. "Let's hope the little chap doesn't have a nervous breakdown." Bertha turned and made for the door again. "Abnormal, that's what it is," she muttered as she stalked out.

Mr. John grinned. "Don't be offended," he told me. "Golden hamsters that write books really do take a bit of getting used to."

"You see, my friend?" Sir William said loftily, when Mr. John had retired to his room. "Even common folk like Bertha think your brain will be overtaxed by all this book-writing of yours."

If there's anything I detest, it's housekeepers and tomcats sounding off about hamsters that write books.

"Peeing on the floor, that's all she thinks we're good for," Enrico said resentfully.

"She doesn't know we make up rhymes and skits," said Caruso.

"Thoroughly professional ones too," said Enrico. "But all anyone ever talks about is Freddy's books."

If there's anything I detest still more, it's guinea pigs

moaning about housekeepers and tomcats sounding off about hamsters that write books.

"Come on, you guys," I said, "your rhymes and skits aren't in the same league as my —"

"Shh!" Sir William had pricked up his ears.

"WHAT'S THAT?"

I could hear it now too, a rustling, fluttering sound. It was coming from outside the window, which was open.

Enrico sat up and listened. "W-what can it be?"

Caruso had also sat up. "It s-sounds like . . ." He broke off.

The fluttering sound grew louder.

Enrico's and Caruso's teeth started to chatter. I had also risen on my haunches, fur bristling, and was staring up at the open window.

Just then, something blotted out the light.

It was a buzzard.

CHaPTER FiVE

I FROZE.

I mean, I really froze. My mental command center, which had registered the image of a buzzard in flight, knocked me over in a flash. Remaining still was my only chance of escaping detection by the huge bird of prey.

Lay THeRe Like a Dead THiNG.

But I could hear.

And I heard Enrico and Caruso scuttle off in different directions, squeaking frantically.

They didn't hide in the cage Bertha had found for them, which would have been the most logical course of action, nor did they play possum. They ran back and forth across the room as if demented, squeaking so shrilly that the sound went right through me.

It was clear that their own mental command centers had gone completely haywire in these unfamiliar surroundings. Meantime, the buzzard continued to

51

flutter outside the window, its dark shape silhouetted against the light.

As I lay there, absolutely still, I heard Enrico and Caruso becoming more and more panic-stricken. At this rate, they would soon end up in the buzzard's talons.

All at once, however, another silhouette appeared at the window.

Then came a ripping sound. Something went whooshing through the air and landed with a thud. Silence fell.

"All clear, my friends," said Sir William. "It was only a kite."

My command center slowly unlocked my limbs. "IT Was WHaT?" I said incredulously.

"A paper kite," said

Sir William, who was sitting on the windowsill. He spread his paws. "The kind that can easily be ripped to shreds by a tomcat's claws."

My command center had now released its hold completely. I turned to look at Enrico and Caruso.

They were sitting up on their haunches some distance apart.

"You mean," Enrico said slowly, "that it wasn't a real buzzard?"

Sir William nodded. "Somebody was flying a kite. It only looked like a buzzard."

Enrico and Caruso glanced at each other. "Sir William," said Caruso, "did you happen to see who that somebody was?"

"I didn't just *happen* to see who it was," said Sir William. "I made a point of looking. It was" — he inserted a pause — "that boy Sebastian."

"But we could have had a heart attack!" squealed Enrico. "WE COULD HAVE DIED OF FRIGHT!"

Caruso chimed in. "Take it easy, you guys," I said soothingly, but they didn't seem to hear.

"We'll teach him a lesson," Enrico said, very calm all of a sudden.

"We'll think of something," said Caruso, just as calmly, "— something he'll never forget. Come on, Enrico." And they retired to their cage.

"Oh dear," said Sir William, who had jumped off the windowsill and joined me, "I've never seen them like this before. They obviously mean that threat seriously. What do you think, old boy? Should we intervene?"

I shook my head. "I can't believe they'd really do anything nasty to him. Besides, they'll have forgotten all about it in an hour."

BUT I WASN'T TOO SURE.

Nothing came of the storm that had been brewing in the distance, and I was eager to get back to work on "The Lord of the Ferrets."

Although my paws hadn't twitched again, as if they were trying to type, I felt certain that my writer's block had disappeared — or *would* disappear if only I could get started.

At the moment, however, there seemed no prospect of this.

Mr. John would first have to unpack the laptop and set it up on the table, quite apart from installing my little rope ladder. He reappeared just as Annabelle, who was back from her piano lesson, came to invite him to have tea with the family.

"I'm afraid I can't invite you animals," she said. "Daddy and Bertha disapprove of sharing their meals with hamsters, cats, and guinea pigs." She looked around inquiringly. "Where are Enrico and Caruso?"

I pointed to their cage. "You mean they're asleep?" Annabelle said. "In the daytime? Well, I expect the journey was pretty stressful for them."

I could only nod, not having the laptop handy, but even if I'd had it I wouldn't have alarmed her by telling her what had stressed them and what they planned to do about it.

"Anyway," she went on, "I'm afraid you can't take your meals with us, but you can naturally have the run of the castle." The stairs were so shallow, she said, they wouldn't present any problem to Enrico and Caruso, let alone Sir William. "As for you," she told me, "you'll simply have to ride on pussyback." So saying, she went off for tea with Mr. John.

I was entranced. Not only by Annabelle's personal aroma of chamomile blossom, but because she'd used the word *pussyback*. Being as small as I am, I can only climb stairs and cover long distances by clinging to the back of Sir William's neck with my teeth and letting him carry me. In one of the Freddy books, this mode of travel had been described as "riding on pussyback." It was only one word among tens of thousands, but Annabelle had remembered it! Could any author have wished for a more attentive reader?

I couldn't wait to hear what she thought of "The

Lord of the Ferrets," but first I would have to finish it. All I could do for now was curl up in my borrowed cage and try to get some sleep.

It was nine minutes to midnight when I woke up (we golden hamsters have as accurate a sense of time as an astronomical chronometer — well, almost as accurate). It didn't surprise me I'd slept for so long. For one thing, I was suffering from jet lag; for another, I hadn't had a chance to sleep all day, and Enrico and Caruso weren't the only ones who'd been stressed by the "buzzard."

BUT WHAT WAS THAT? My nest was bathed in flickering, bluish-green light. I darted outside, and there, in the middle of the big table beside the window, I saw the laptop. Its screen had been folded back and

switched on, and my little rope ladder was dangling from the edge of the table.

MANY THANKS, MR. JOHN!

The room was so quiet, my ears could detect the laptop's almost inaudible hum. I couldn't see a sign of Sir William, who was probably asleep in Mr. John's room, his usual custom. Enrico and Caruso were slumbering in their cage (or so I assumed. Where else would they be at this late hour?). Ideal conditions, Mr. Author!

I clambered swiftly onto the table, hurried over to the laptop, and retrieved "The Lord of the Ferrets." Just as it came up on the screen, my paws started twitching. As soon as I'd reread what I'd written to date, away they went.

> The ferrets were exceptionally large — almost as long as a man's arm — and had thick, yellowish fur. They opened their mouths so wide, one could see past their needle-sharp teeth and down their throats. And issuing from those throats came a snarl. It was such a piercing, ferocious snarl that . . .

I stopped to listen. All was quiet.

> . . . that it seemed impossible they would obey their master.

But the tall, fierce-faced man whom the villagers called Grim Harry, on account of his gloomy demeanor, muttered, "Hush, Cruncher! Hush, Muncher! Hush, the two of you!"

And the ferrets instantly stopped snarling.

Grim Harry put them down beside the rabbit hole he had left uncovered by a net. "Hush," he repeated, and they sat quite still in front of it.

Next he took two bell collars from a linen bag slung over his shoulder. They were made of leather, and each had two or three bells on it. He stooped and buckled them around the ferrets' necks, then straightened up.

"Off you go, Cruncher! You too, Muncher!"

The ferrets shook themselves, and the bells jangled discordantly. They were sounding the death knell for more than a dozen rabbits.

Then the ferrets disappeared down the rabbit hole.

As for what would happen inside the warren . . .

"Help! Help!"

I sat up with a start.

"HELP! HELP!"

No, that hadn't come from my story. It hadn't come from here in the room either, but from farther away. The voice was high-pitched — loud and piercing.

Suddenly, the light went on in Mr. John's room. A moment later he came thundering down the stairs in his bathrobe with Sir William bounding after him.

"Sir William!" I called.

Sir William leaped onto the table and I climbed on his back. "Hang on tight with your teeth, old boy," he said, and we went racing after Mr. John.

The spiral staircase came out in a long landing. Bertha, with her hair in curlers, had just turned on the light when Lord Templeton appeared too.

The cries ceased.

"**QUICK!**" Bertha said breathlessly. "That was one of the children!"

She hurried off with Lord Templeton and Mr. John at her heels. Sir William and I brought up the rear. We turned off down a passage and came to the open door of a bedroom. Bertha glanced inside and hurried on. Through another open door, and we found ourselves in Sebastian's room.

He was cowering down in bed, staring at his right arm.

Blood was oozing from it.

CHAPTER SIX

ANNABELLE WAS STANDING beside Sebastian's bed. She turned to us and said, "He's bleeding. Something bit him."

"It was those guinea pigs!" Sebastian bawled.

THOSE GUINEA PIGS BIT ME!"

"Let me see, boy." Bertha examined his arm. "Hmm, two bites. Not very deep, luckily. You've just had a tetanus jab. That's lucky too."

Lord Templeton knit his brow. "What do you think?" he asked Mr. John.

Mr. John had also examined Sebastian's arm. "I think it's most unlikely these bites were inflicted by Enrico and Caruso."

"But it *was* them!" roared Sebastian. "They snarled and they bit me!"

"Guinea pigs are peaceful creatures," said Mr. John. "They only bite when subjected to extreme stress."

Sebastian suddenly subsided. He stole a quick glance at something in the corner of his room: the torn and broken remains of the kite that resembled a buzzard. He eyed the bite marks on his arm and said no more.

"Well, if you ask me," Bertha declared, "they look more like rat bites." She turned to Lord Templeton. "The floors here are riddled with holes. You really ought to get the old place restored."

"By all means," Lord Templeton retorted curtly, "if you'll foot the bill. And now, that's enough excitement for one night. Whatever bit the boy — rats,

guinea pigs, or whatever — we'll look into it tomorrow."

Sir William sniffed the air. "Do you smell that, my friend?" he whispered to me. "That's no rat."

I could smell it too. It was the unmistakable scent of Enrico and Caruso.

When we got back to the tower, Mr. John went over to the guinea pigs' cage. "Enrico?" he called. "Caruso?"

No sign of movement. Mr. John reached into the cage and cautiously lifted the lid of the shoe box that served Enrico and Caruso as a bedroom — another of Bertha's ideas.

IT WaS EMPTY.

Mr. John looked at me and Sir William. "Kids, I'm relying on you to help me solve this case. Good night." And he went upstairs to his room.

"Good heavens!" said Sir William. "Who would have thought our likable twosome capable of such an atrocity? I confess I'm rather disappointed in them — as animals,

I mean,
not as entertainers."

"I still find it hard to believe." I shook
my head. "But the evidence against them is quite
overwhelming."

"No, it isn't," I heard Enrico say, and Caruso added,
"Everything points that way, we know, but it wasn't us
who bit the boy." They came sidling through the door,
which was ajar.

"You *were* in his room, though," said Sir William.

They nodded. "It was like this," said Enrico. "We were
outside his door, wondering how to get in . . ."

"We wanted to scare him with our realistic
impression of a snarling ferret," Caruso put in.

". . . when he started calling for help. Annabelle

came running, so we sneaked in behind her and hid under the bed."

"We only wanted to find out what had happened," said Caruso. "The rest you know."

"Hmm," I said, and Sir William shook his head.

At that, they solemnly raised their right forepaws. "We swear by all that's sacred: We didn't bite Sebastian."

Was *anything* sacred to those guinea pigs? I wondered. "Even supposing you really didn't bite him," I said, "**WHO DID?**"

"Quite so," said Sir William. "That's just the point. Until we discover who inflicted those bites, I'm afraid they're down to you."

The room was silent once more. Enrico and Caruso had retired to their cage in a sulk and Sir William had disappeared upstairs. I was seated on the table, feeling thoroughly chipper, with the laptop faintly humming away in front of me.

Was there any reason why I shouldn't go on with my story? Absolutely none.

The ferrets shook themselves, and the bells jangled discordantly. They were sounding the death knell for more than a dozen rabbits.

Then the ferrets disappeared down the hole.

As for what would happen inside the warren . . .

. . . Grim Harry could picture it in his mind's eye. He knew that he had trained his ferrets well, and that he could depend on them to do their job. They would flush out the rabbits, stampede them with their vicious snarls and jangling bells, and drive them along the tunnels to the surface. They would bite them too, but they were not allowed to kill them — not under any circumstances. Dead rabbits remained belowground and blocked the tunnels. Then the hunt would be over.

Grim Harry waited for the first rabbits to become entangled in the nets draped over the exit tunnels.

He could not, even had he wished to, imagine how terrified and panic-stricken those rabbits were feeling. . . .

"Freddy?"

I gave a start.

My astronomically accurate sense of time told me that it was precisely six minutes past seven in the morning — roughly the hour at which I was always immersed in my first deep sleep of the day.

"FREDDY!"

I crawled out of my nest. Sir William's huge black form was looming over the cage. "Sorry to wake you, old boy, but it's urgent."

What could be so urgent at six minutes past seven in the morning that he had to disturb a golden hamster's

first deep sleep of the day?
I yawned and stretched.
"What is it?" I asked
drowsily.

"I was taking a little morning stroll earlier on," said Sir William, "and on the edge of a field behind a barn —"

"You go strolling behind barns at this hour of the day?"

"Well, I was feeling like a bite of fresh breakfast."

I stared at him. **FRESH** breakfast? My civilized feline friend had actually gone on a mouse hunt! Back home he ate canned food off a plate, but once in the country he turned into a bone-crunching predator. Well, fair enough. I'm extremely civilized myself, but I dearly love to crunch live mealworms. (Incidental note: If my readers are interested in a personal tip, there's nothing more scrumptious than a mealworm's pale yellow innards.) Anyway, Sir William was welcome to his fresh mouse breakfast. At that particular moment, however, I found it reassuring that he and I were separated by the stout bars of my cage.

"And behind this barn," Sir William went on, "I was suddenly accosted."

"Accosted? By whom?"

"By a deputation."

"What do you mean, a deputation?"

"A deputation of animals requesting my help."

Twenty minutes later we were behind the barn. "This business affects us all," Sir William told me, so he'd woken Enrico and Caruso, who were also asleep (*still* asleep, I mean, not *just* asleep like me). "It affects you rodents in particular," he'd added, but that was all we could get out of him. "Wait and see," he said mysteriously, so we waited.

But there was nothing to be seen.

Nothing, at least, that resembled a deputation. Between the barn and the neighboring turnip field was a strip of land overgrown with bramble bushes, and beneath them, invisible from the air, a number of holes could be discerned in the loamy soil. These holes were of a size that would have enabled Caruso to enter them with ease. It's a trifle embarrassing for me to have to admit this, but the sight of them meant absolutely nothing to me. I was still half asleep, I guess, but sufficiently awake to keep an eye on them.

And then, from one of the holes, a nose protruded. A brownish nose adorned with tremulous whiskers, it protruded farther, sniffing the air, until the whole head came into view. The long ears proclaimed that they belonged to — what else? **— a RaBBiT.** The creature cautiously emerged from the hole and sat up, ears pricked and swiveling in all directions. Then it turned to face the hole. "Y-you, y-you . . ." it stammered. Suddenly, it gave a gigantic leap sideways. "You can come out now!" it called without a stammer.

It was a while before the next rabbit emerged. Having done so with great deliberation, it looked around condescendingly with its nose in the air and the corners of its mouth turned down, as if to say, "**WHaT'S aLL THE FUSS aBOUT?**" The third rabbit, which appeared a moment later, neither stammered nor put its nose in the air. Unlike the first two, it was a girl rabbit.

"Permit me to make the introductions." Sir William indicated the newcomers with a semicircular sweep of the paw. "In order of appearance: Nibbles, Marmaduke, and Lucinda."

"In order of seniority would have been preferable," Marmaduke said grandly. "I'm a stickler for etiquette."

Sir William's eyes narrowed, but he made no comment. "These," he said, pointing to us, "are the friends I told you about: Freddy, Enrico, and Caruso."

"Charmed, I'm sure." Marmaduke looked down his nose at us, conveying an impression of extreme boredom.

"T-two . . . t-two . . ." Nibbles stopped short. Then he gave a sideways leap and completed the sentence without difficulty: "Two guinea pigs and a hamster! How fascinating!"

"Pleased to meet you," Lucinda said with a smile.

"I would suggest," said Sir William, "that you simply tell my friends the facts of the matter."

"Very well, so be it." Marmaduke cleared his throat self-importantly. "In the course of last night, our colony came under attack."

"T-two . . . t-two . . ." Nibbles gave a backward leap. "Two predators invaded our warren in the middle of the night! They snarled and tried to bite us!"

"Ferrets, they were," said Lucinda. "You can imagine the result, I'm sure. Four of us nearly died of fright."

"Most regrettable," said Sir William. He turned to Enrico and Caruso. "You realize what this means from your point of view? That boy Sebastian was bitten by ferrets."

They nodded, beaming delightedly, and Enrico said, "So we're off the hook."

I didn't share that view at all. There was an important piece of circumstantial evidence that Sir William seemed to have overlooked, curiously enough, but I temporarily chose not to point this out. "Had you posted a sentry?" I asked the rabbits.

"That goes without saying, my dear sir." Marmaduke looked down his nose at me (no great feat, given the purely physical difference in size between a rabbit and a golden hamster). "But the neglectful creature was obviously asleep."

"I . . . I . . ." Nibbles performed another jump. This time he shot straight upward like a rocket. "I wasn't!" he cried. "I'm *renowned* for my devotion to duty!"

"I BELIEVE HIM," said Lucinda, "and so do most of us. But that poses a question: How did the ferrets manage to get in unnoticed?" She paused. Then she said, "Whatever route they took, Nibbles would have been bound to smell them."

CHAPTER SEVEN

THAT WAS JUST IT.

A ferret's scent is so strong, even humans can smell it. As for the highly sensitive nose of a rabbit, it couldn't have failed to register it. I'll refrain from discoursing on the supreme sensitivity of a hamster's nose and simply say this: I hadn't caught the slightest whiff of ferret in Sebastian's room.

I glanced at Enrico and Caruso, but their innocent expressions conveyed that Lucinda's statement had no bearing on them. And Sir William? He too seemed to have missed the point. Not for the first time, it would be up to me to give him a helping hand.

"It was all very mysterious," Lucinda was saying. She shivered suddenly. The poor thing was frightened, I realized.

Of course she was frightened. Lucinda, Nibbles, Marmaduke — all three were absolutely terrified. They were trying to conceal the fact, not from us but from themselves. If they had admitted their fear, they would have panicked, and that would have sealed their fate.

But Lucinda had recovered her composure. "They disappeared as mysteriously as they had appeared," she said. "All of a sudden, they were gone."

"Hmm," said Sir William, "that really is mysterious. Whatever the truth, we must now work out what we can do to help you."

"What's to work out?" said Enrico. "It's as clear as daylight."

"Oh?"

"Yes," said Caruso, nodding. "The rabbits must be protected."

"True," said Sir William. "The only problem is, I can't stand guard here day and night."

"You've no need to," said Enrico.

"We'll do it," said Caruso.

"**JUST a MINUTE.**" I stared at them. "Do what, exactly?"

"We'll take on the job of guarding the rabbits," Enrico said, looking as if he really meant it.

"We'll move into their warren." Caruso was also looking deadly serious. "If the ferrets come back, we'll chase them away."

"And how do you propose to do that?" I asked, trying to inject a good dose of sarcasm into my tone. "By scaring them off with your realistic snarls? By biting them, maybe?"

"You found us pretty convincing yourself on one occasion," said Enrico.

"When the chips are down," declared Caruso, "we turn into fearless warriors."

I was growing exasperated. "DON'T BE RIDICULOUS! YOU—"

"Freddy!" Sir William looked at me sharply. "I think we can safely delegate the protection of our newfound friends to Enrico and Caruso. Agreed?"

What else could I do but nod? I'd been outvoted yet again. I washed my hands of the whole affair. Those conceited guinea pigs were merely hoping to drum up an audience for their skits. They were even prepared to do battle with ferrets for the sake of their art — unless, of course, they planned to perform for the ferrets themselves.

"Y-you m-mean . . . Y-you m-mean . . ." Nibbles leaped toward Enrico and Caruso. "You mean you're fearless warriors? How exciting!"

"Your request is granted, gentlemen," drawled Marmaduke. "We graciously permit you to enter our service."

Lucinda smiled at Enrico and Caruso. "Thank you," she said simply. "I suggest we introduce you to the others."

The rabbits took leave of me and Sir William and disappeared down the hole with Enrico and Caruso in their wake.

Sir William watched them go. "Nitwit," he muttered.

"What?" I thought I must have misheard. "Who do you mean?"

"That pompous Marmaduke. HE'S OFF HIS ROCKER."

"Yes," I said, "but Nibbles is also a few lettuce leaves short of a salad."

"True." Sir William grinned. "So sixty-six and two-thirds of that deputation were a trifle . . . er, cracked."

"Listen, you two." Lucinda squeezed out of the rabbit hole and came hopping over to us. "You don't by any chance . . ." She paused and looked back, then lowered her voice. "You don't by any chance have a little celery on you, do you?"

"A little *what?*"

"**CELERY.**" Lucinda's eyes shone. "**CELERY,**" she chanted suddenly. "**CELERY, CELERY, CELERY, LOVELY CELERY.** But there isn't any here. You don't have some on you, do you?"

"Er, no. So sorry."

"Really not?"

"Really not, my dear." Sir William shook his head apologetically. "We didn't come prepared for such a request, I fear."

"A pity." Lucinda turned away, her lop ears drooping sadly. "Why can I never get hold of any lovely celery?" And she disappeared down the hole.

"A hundred percent cracked," chuckled Sir William. "A hundred percent precisely."

On the way back to the castle, Sir William went bounding across the courtyard with me on his back. When we stopped I asked him, "Did you smell anything in Sebastian's room last night? Aside from Enrico and Caruso, I mean?"

"No, just them," he said. "Nothing resembling the scent of a ferret, if that's what you're getting at."

He fell silent for a while. Then he said, "I'm now pretty sure it was Enrico and Caruso that bit the boy. If so, (a) they're capable of biting, and (b) they've got something to atone for. That's why we can safely leave them to guard the rabbits."

Hmm. A wise decision. "What shall we tell Mr. John?" I asked.

"That Sebastian's bites were inflicted by ferrets, what else?"

Another wise decision.

I might have made it myself.

✳ ✳ ✳

Grim Harry decided to return home by way of a secluded path through the forest, even though he risked running into one of the Baron's gamekeepers, if not the Baron himself. He had not committed any crime, it was true, but the Baron made the laws and sat in judgment of those who broke them. Although Grim Harry knew from past experience that it was unwise to rely on a clear-cut distinction between what was lawful and unlawful, taking the path through the forest would enable him to reach his hut on the edge of the village unobserved. The villagers could not be allowed to see how many rabbits he had caught. If he sold them one by one, claiming that his bag had been meager, it would drive up the price.

In fact, it was a long time since he had caught so many rabbits at once. His nets had trapped no less than sixteen, and he was carrying them on a long pole over his right shoulder. Suspended from his left shoulder were the nets and, on a leather strap, the box containing the ferrets.

Grim Harry had just passed the massive beech tree that had been struck by lightning the previous year, when he came to a halt. Had a horse snorted somewhere nearby?

He listened intently . . .

I paused and looked up. Had something creaked?

I had been interrupted so often while writing "The Lord of the Ferrets" (every time, now come to think of it) that another interruption would have come as no surprise to me. But all was still — and why not? It was nearly one in the morning and everyone else was asleep. I myself had slept soundly all day, only to be woken late that afternoon by a thunderstorm. Mr. John had shut the window because of the rain, so the room was rather stuffy, but I felt as chipper and wide-awake as — well, as any hamster feels at night.

He listened intently.

And then, from around a bend in the path, a horseman rode into view.

It was the Baron.

For a moment, Grim Harry felt tempted to dart behind the trunk of the beech tree, but he was encumbered by the rabbits, and besides, the Baron had already caught sight of him.

Behind the Baron came his young son, riding a pony, followed on foot by a gamekeeper.

Grim Harry put his rabbit-laden pole on the ground and performed the deep obeisance expected of all the Baron's underlings. The horses came to a halt just short of him.

"A goodly bag you have there," said the Baron.

Grim Harry continued to bow from the waist but could picture the Baron looking down at him, a corpulent, powerfully built figure mounted on a huge stallion.

"Fortune smiled on me today, Your Lordship," said Grim Harry.

"Is he allowed to hunt here, Father?" That was the petulant voice of the Baron's young son. "Surely the game in the fields and forest belongs to us?"

At that, Grim Harry straightened up. He stood there, tall and fierce-faced, gazing at the Baron's son. It was such a keen, piercing gaze that the boy looked away. "Rabbits are fair game, Your Lordship," said Grim Harry. "Hunting them has been lawful since time immemorial — as lawful as the gathering of mushrooms and berries."

"Down, fellow! Bow low!" The gamekeeper lunged at him. "Would you deny His Lordship the deference due to him?"

"Leave him be," commanded the Baron, and, to Grim Harry: "You're right, rabbits are fair game." He paused. "But only if they be hunted without a weapon." He pointed to the box slung from Grim Harry's shoulder. "Are those your ferrets? You use them for hunting?"

"I do, Your Lordship."

The Baron eyed the box with a thoughtful air. Abruptly, he wheeled his horse and rode off.

"But, Father . . ."

"Come!"

The Baron, his son, and the gamekeeper disappeared around the next bend in the path through the forest.

Grim Harry . . .

What was that? I sat up straight.

It was blowing a gale outside and raining hard. It sounded like a regular downpour. Never mind . . .

Grim Harry stood staring after them. He felt uneasy. The Baron was up to something, but what? Thoughtfully, he picked up his carrying pole. . . .

The rain was rattling against the window.

It wasn't raining, it was hailing, and very hard at that. The hailstones must have been as big as pigeons' eggs. Boy oh boy, it was positively alarming! I hoped the windowpanes would hold up.

. I looked at the laptop's screen. No, there wasn't any point, not under these conditions. I saved what I'd written. Just then . . .

"Help! Help!"

I froze.

"Help! Help!"

The cries were coming from some place way off, and the voice was high-pitched — loud and piercing.

No doubt about it:  **THE VOICE WAS SEBASTIAN'S.**

CHAPTER EIGHT

SEBASTIAN WAS STANDING up in bed.

He was cowering in a corner with the rumpled pillows at his feet, trembling convulsively. He had stopped screaming, but he was still staring straight through us — staring as if he could see some frightful apparition in the middle of the room.

The bandage around his arm had slipped, but I couldn't detect any fresh blood.

"There, there, Sebastian," Bertha was saying in her calm, deep voice. She had already said it several times. "There, there," she repeated.

Slowly, like someone awakening from a trance, Sebastian tore his gaze away from the invisible cause of his terror. His trembling subsided. He slid down the wall and collapsed on the bed. Annabelle put her arm around him, and he started to weep.

91

"There, there," Bertha said gruffly, taking his hand. Sebastian wept all the harder.

"Can you smell anything, old boy?" Sir William whispered to me.

"No," I whispered back. "Neither Enrico and Caruso, nor ferrets, nor any other unusual scent."

Sir William nodded. With me on his back, he had positioned himself behind Lord Templeton and Mr. John but to one side, where we could follow everything closely. All was quiet outside the window. The prodigious hailstorm had lasted less than a minute.

Sebastian's wails were gradually giving way to sobs.

"What was it, my boy?" asked Lord Templeton. "Was it a bad dream?"

Sebastian shook his head. "It wasn't a dream, Daddy."
He stared fearfully at the middle of the room. "He
was real."

"He?"

a MaN—a huge man, and all dressed up in
old-fashioned clothes like the ones in my book about
the Middle Ages." Sebastian shuddered. "He had an awful
gray face. Almost green, it was."

"How could you see all that so clearly in the dark?"

"I turned on the light at once."

"It was on," Annabelle confirmed. "The bedside light
was on when I came in."

"I thought it was just my imagination, and he'd
disappear if I turned on the light. But he didn't, he just
stared at me. His eyes seemed to go right through me. . . .
And his hoarse breathing . . ." Sebastian shuddered again.
"He was real!" he cried suddenly. "Honestly, he was!"

"There, there," Bertha said again.

"And what happened to the man?" Mr. John asked. "I
mean, where did he go?"

"He vanished. I don't know how, but all at once he wasn't there anymore." Sebastian looked at the window. "It was just when the hail started."

I wish I could say I saw the light at this stage, but to be frank, I was completely in the dark. Some things are

so improbable that even a razor-sharp brain like mine
fails to grasp them.

"And then I started shouting."

"Well, well," said Lord Templeton, "that was a really
bad dream."

"But I *wasn't* dreaming," Sebastian insisted. "The man
was real."

"Real or not," said Bertha, "I don't suppose you feel
like spending the rest of the night in here."

Sebastian certainly didn't. Bertha and Annabelle
decided to put up a cot for him in Annabelle's room.

We returned to our room in the tower, and Mr. John
disappeared up the stairs with a "See you tomorrow, kids."

Sir William was about to follow when Enrico and
Caruso came dashing in.

"You two?!" Sir William fixed them with a green-eyed glare. "Why aren't you at your post?"

"Because they've gone!" Enrico said breathlessly.

"**THE FERRETS!**" Caruso blurted out. "They were there!"

"Easy, easy." Sir William sat down. "Begin at the beginning, please."

"Okay." Enrico drew a deep breath. "It was like this: When we finally reached the warren, we found the rabbits down in the dumps."

"Their morale was at rock bottom, so to speak," Caruso amplified.

"Let me guess," I said. "You performed one of your skits, and their morale went through the roof."

Enrico looked hurt. "If you know everything already, we may as well save our breath."

"Freddy, please." Sir William gave me a reproving little shake of the head. "As for you two," he told the guinea pigs, "kindly get to the point."

"Okay," said Caruso, "we'll give you the shortened version." And he and Enrico described how, after completing their morale-boosting operation, they'd organized the warren's defenses in an exemplary manner. Each rabbit hole was assigned a sentry who stationed himself just inside the entrance. They themselves occupied a command post in the heart of the warren. "I mean," said Enrico, "how could the two of us have guarded *all* the tunnels?"

An uncharitable listener (and I'm nothing if not charitable) might have come up with a different interpretation: Instead of protecting their charges, they had simply reversed the process and protected themselves from the ferrets by stationing rabbits all over the place.

"But in spite of that," said Caruso, "the ferrets suddenly appeared. They appeared out of nowhere, so to speak, right in the middle of the warren."

"In the middle of the warren?" Sir William repeated. "What do you mean?"

"What we say. Right in the chamber where we were." Enrico shivered. "Compared to that, the sudden appearance of a buzzard is as dramatic as a housefly landing on a bowl of sugar."

"But why didn't the sentries sound the alarm?" I asked. "The ferrets must have gone past them." In a suitably sarcastic tone, I added, "Or did they materialize into flesh and blood before your very eyes?"

"You've hit the nail on the head."

"MEANING WHAT?"

"They really did materialize into flesh and blood before our very eyes," said Enrico. "We watched them take shape."

Silence.

Sir William and I exchanged a glance.

"You're welcome to think we're nuts," said Caruso. "We don't mind."

"But you'd be wrong," Enrico said. "For one thing, because we aren't nuts, and, for another, because none of us would ever get to the bottom of this ferret business."

"Very well." Sir William sighed. "Let's assume it's true. What happened next?"

"It was horrible," Caruso said with an involuntary shiver. "The ferrets were enormous. They opened their mouths and snarled at us, but **'SNARLED'** is a pale description. It sounded like a hurricane."

"What scared me most of all," said Enrico, who was also shivering, "were their collars."

"Their collars?" I said.

"Yes. There were bells on them. They made a terribly discordant, jangling sound."

That was when a bell started ringing in my head.

"But there was something else," said Caruso, still shivering. "The smell!"

"Well," I said, "ferrets have a strong scent, everyone knows that."

"That's just it," said Enrico. "These ferrets had no scent. No scent at all."

I would gladly have called the guinea pigs insane, but I couldn't — not anymore. Too many things were starting to fall into place. It was like doing a jigsaw puzzle. The first few pieces had fit together easily, but I still didn't know what the puzzle depicted.

"They drove us into a corner," Caruso recounted, "and we realized we were doomed."

MEAN REALLY DOOMED," Enrico put a paw over his eyes. "I can still recall what flashed through my mind: Enrico, you've lived life to the fullest. You've made the most of your artistic talents and —"

"Yes, yes," Sir William cut in. "It must have been a most unpleasant predicament, but I'm anxious to know how you managed to resolve it."

"We didn't."

"I'm sorry?"

"We didn't resolve it," said Enrico. "It resolved itself, so to speak."

"Because the ferrets suddenly vanished," said Caruso. "They literally dissolved into thin air before our eyes."

I had to ask a certain question, that was clear as daylight, but I hesitated. What if the answer confirmed my suspicions? What would happen next? I didn't know, but one thing I did know for certain: There was trouble ahead **—a GREAT DEAL OF TROUBLE.**

I drew a deep breath. "Exactly when did the ferrets disappear? I mean, is there something that fixes the time in your mind?"

Enrico and Caruso nodded, as if they'd been expecting the question. Enrico said, "The ferrets vanished just as something happened outside."

And Caruso added, "It was just when that big hailstorm started."

Okay, Freddy, once more from the beginning.

Dawn was breaking, and I was still sitting beside my nest. It was a considerable time since Sir William had retired to his blanket and Enrico and Caruso to their cage. All three of them were completely at a loss. What were they to make of ferrets that looked like flesh and blood but appeared and disappeared like disembodied spirits? I hadn't told them of my suspicions.

WHY NOT? Because first I had to get them clear in my mind. The trouble was, the longer I debated them, the more improbable they seemed. All right, once more from the beginning:

Point 1: I'd been working on "The Lord of the Ferrets." I'd stopped writing when the hailstorm started.

Point 2: While I was writing, a man resembling Grim Harry had appeared to Sebastian. He had vanished when the hailstorm started.

Point 3: At the same time as I was writing, two ferrets closely resembling Cruncher and Muncher had appeared in the rabbit warren. They'd disappeared when the hailstorm started.

If I played dumb and applied the laws of logic (by assuming that such coincidences meant something), there was only one possible conclusion:

ENEVER I WROTE, IT ENABLED GRIM ARRY AND HIS FERRETS TO APPEAR.

Whenever I stopped writing, they disappeared again.

What had been happening the night Sebastian got bitten? I'd also been writing, and it was when I resumed work on my story that the ferrets had made their first appearance in the rabbit warren.

And earlier on? What had happened when I was working on "The Lord of the Ferrets" back home? Could it be that Great-Aunt Agatha too had died because . . . ?

At this point I stopped thinking and crawled into my nest. But even when I curled up and tried to sleep, the same thought recurred: I must find out for sure. That was as far as it went.

Something inside me refused to pursue the subject further.

After all, it was hard to admit to myself that we were in a terrible predicament.

Why? Because someone who is genuinely determined to kill people tends to succeed.

Especially when that someone is a bloodthirsty ghost.

CHapter Nine

IT WAS LATE AFTERNOON when I awoke.

Enrico and Caruso had returned to their post in the rabbit warren. Sir William thought this admirably courageous of them. "I couldn't defend them against those fearsome beasts down there," he said, "whereas here I could."

I made no comment, not wanting to alarm him unnecessarily. If those ferocious ferrets were anywhere near as big as I imagined them to be, not even Sir William would stand a chance against them.

Enrico and Caruso realized this too, so they preferred to await their fate in the warren, where they could clown around and revel in the rabbits' acclaim.

"Sir William," I said, "I have a favor to ask."

"Spit it out, old boy."

"Could you go and get Annabelle — and leave me alone with her?"

"OHO!" Sir William winked at me. "Not thinking of cheating on little Sophie, are you?"

WHaT a THOROUGHLY UNCaLLED-FOR REMaRK!

It was no concern of his that Annabelle smelled divinely of chamomile blossom, or that she had read all the Freddy books with the closest attention. Besides, I had something quite different in mind. "Would you be so kind?" I said, controlling myself with an effort.

"Of course, old boy." Sir William set off, but not without giving me another wink. My only response was a shrug of the shoulders, but I was seething inside. Okay, I told myself, cool it!

Sir William naturally found it child's play to show Annabelle what he wanted by mewing and plucking at her skirt (the cat has yet to be born that can't make a human dance to its tune), and when she walked into the tower room and called, "Hi,

Freddy!," smelling divinely of — but I think I'm repeating myself. Anyway, I'd taken up my position on the table beside the open laptop.

As soon as Sir William had left the room again, I typed, *Hi, Annabelle. I'd like a word with you about something. It's a pretty wild theory of mine, and I don't want to make a fool of myself in front of the others. Can we keep it to ourselves?*

Annabelle nodded. "Of course," she said, sitting down on the chair beside the table.

It's about that man Sebastian saw.

"You don't think it was a dream? You think he really saw him?"

That's precisely what I think. The man was a kind of apparition, and I suspect that Sebastian isn't the only person who has seen him. I have no idea how real the man is, or whether he's capable of actually doing things. Bad things, for instance. Then I typed, *From the look of it, I'm the one who conjures him up.*

"YOU ARE?"

Yes. I began by telling Annabelle about "The Lord of the Ferrets."

Then I described what had happened in the rabbit warren and told her what conclusion I'd come to: that Grim Harry and his ferrets appeared whenever I worked on my story, and that they disappeared whenever I stopped.

Annabelle had been following my account on the screen with one hand over her mouth. "Are you certain of this?" she asked.

Not altogether, I typed. *There's still a chance I'm wrong.* I hesitated. *When exactly did your great-aunt die?*

Annabelle didn't have to think for long. "Three weeks ago. Friday night, it was."

In other words, the night Enrico and Caruso had scared me by snarling like ferrets — the night I'd begun to write my story. This had split the chances of my being wrong in half.

And when did she borrow the Freddy books from you?

"Three days earlier, on Tuesday morning. I know that for certain, because I went into town with Bertha immediately afterward."

That was it: No chance of a mistake. I had planned my story on the Monday night. I drew a deep breath. *Annabelle,* I typed, *Grim Harry must have appeared to your great-aunt on the Monday night and commanded her to invite us all to the castle. That's why she borrowed your Freddy books and wrote to Mr. John.*

"You think so?" Annabelle stared at me wide-eyed. "And a few days later?"

That was when . . . I paused, then began again. *That was when he killed her.*

Annabelle stared at the screen in silence. I couldn't tell what she was thinking.

Suddenly, she said, "So the man *can* do bad things. He frightened Great-Aunt Agatha —**HE SCARED HER TO DEATH.**"

109

She nodded. "He didn't want her telling us anything." She lapsed into silence again. Propping her chin on her hands, she gazed at the screen with a frown. I don't know why (perhaps it was her wrinkled brow), but she looked quite a bit older all of a sudden. Even so, I doubted whether she had grasped the crucial point.

After a while she looked up. "Well?" she said. "Were you working on your story both those nights?"

That was the crucial point. I nodded.

"In that case, Freddy, there's only one thing for it." She gazed at me earnestly. "You must stop writing."

I STARED AT HER.

"You mustn't go on with 'The Lord of the Ferrets.'"

But of course! I smote my brow with my forepaw, metaphorically speaking. That was it! Why on earth hadn't I thought of it myself?

On the other hand, was I really expected to abandon my beloved story? What wonderful material! Humans, animals, disembodied spirits, extreme suspense! And there was another factor that merited consideration: I'd already put a lot of work into it.

"Freddy," Annabelle said softly, "what's on your mind?"

I'm mourning for my story, I typed. *But of course I'll abandon it.*

Annabelle nodded contentedly.

But I couldn't refrain from typing **Sigh!!!** on the screen.

My real sigh came later.

Midnight was approaching, and I was sitting in front of the laptop, wide-awake. I pressed the H key followed by the P (Mr. John had installed some programs that enabled me to carry out complicated procedures by pressing a few keys in succession). All I needed to do now was press the return key, and . . . Whoops! I'd come within a hair of opening "The Lord of the Ferrets"!

Would that have been wise? No, Freddy, it wouldn't — in fact, it would have been extremely foolish.

How easily I might have been tempted to resume work on the story!

Okay, "The Lord of the Ferrets" was a dead letter, together with Cruncher and Muncher, the Baron, the Baron's son, the gamekeeper, and all the other people who might have made an appearance. All dead and gone.

But were they really dead? No, not until I'd deleted the whole story. Wipe the slate clean, Freddy!

Very well. I had saved my story as *The Lord of the Ferrets*. I clicked my way down the list to it (Mr. John had attached a mouse to the laptop, though it isn't exactly child's play for a smart but diminutive golden hamster to use it). Then I drew a deep breath and deleted the story.

I really and truly deleted "The Lord of the Ferrets." It was gone, finished, in the trash can.

And then I felt such a stab in the heart, such a pang of

sorrow, that I felt sick. Nauseous, I mean, as if I'd eaten a putrid mealworm. And the worst of it was, the sensation persisted.

It would pass, I told myself. I just had to stick it out for a bit longer. Besides, I ought to erase the backup file as well, right away and without looking at it first. No, Freddy, don't do it! No!

But I did. I'd retrieved the copy before I knew it, because I naturally had to take a look at it for fear of deleting the wrong file. I'd saved the copy as *FSC (Freddy's Secret Copy)* for safety's sake. Yes, that seemed to be it all right. Did it really correspond to the original text? I reread the last paragraph:

Grim Harry stood staring after them. He felt uneasy. The Baron was up to something, but what? Thoughtfully, he picked up his carrying pole . . .

MY PaWS TWiTCHED. I couldn't leave it like that. Every sentence deserves an ending and a period.

Thoughtfully, he picked up his carrying pole, shouldered it, and headed for home.

Freddy! Paws off! You know what'll happen!

Of course I knew. I'd planned my story with care, after all. A good storyteller knows his story *before* he writes it down. Not in detail, of course. The details emerge while he's writing.

If you go on with your story, Freddy, you'll put them all in mortal danger!

Correct. All three of them: Grim Harry, Cruncher, and Muncher. That was the way I'd planned it. After their encounter in the forest, I was going to engineer another meeting between Grim Harry and the Baron. Then Grim Harry would *really* be in danger.

Freddy! Write any more, and you'll conjure up the ferocious ferrets! AND THEIR SINISTER MASTER!

I hoped so, because a story is no good unless it brings the characters to life. But where could the next meeting take place? The Baron and Grim Harry would have to cross swords in front of everyone. Was there any place where high-born and humble, nobleman and peasant, gathered together under the same roof?

And then — I honestly don't know where it came from — a scene took shape in my mind:

Grim Harry did not go to church because he was devout, but because the Baron expected it of all his underlings. It was inadvisable to shirk this duty because His Lordship often attended Sunday worship. Either alone or accompanied by his family, he would sit in the gallery, a massive figure of a man, and survey the congregation with an eagle eye.

Grim Harry looked up at the gallery. This Sunday, the Baron had only brought his daughter with him. A little girl of ten at most, she was attired like a princess in silk and satin. Grim Harry, who suddenly became aware that the Baron was watching him, lowered his gaze. It was best to look submissive in His Lordship's presence.

The parson began his sermon. His subject — "Ye shall fear those set in authority over ye" — had as usual been prescribed by the Baron, for the parson too was an underling of his, and whenever the Baron devised a new law, the parson had to conclude his sermon by reading it aloud from the pulpit. . . .

Hey, was that a sigh I'd heard?

Silence.

THERE! Another sigh . . . Sir William! It must be Sir William asleep on his blanket in the room upstairs. He was dreaming, probably.

All was quiet elsewhere.

I looked at the screen. I had actually written several more lines!

And nothing had happened.

I listened. Nothing to be heard — nothing alarming in any way.

Had Annabelle and I been wrong? Had we seen a connection that didn't exist at all? I looked at the screen again. My description of the scene in the church, at least, had failed to conjure up Grim Harry. Could I venture to write on?

I had a sudden vision of Grim Harry sitting in the pew with his head bowed, the Baron and his little daughter in the gallery, the parson in the pulpit . . .

The sermon dragged on. At last, however, the parson ended it with the words: "So be humble and obedient, for therein lies the key to salvation." He paused. Then he said, "And now, give ear to what our noble and gracious lord has ordained." He picked up a sheet of paper and read the following aloud: "Given the twenty-first day of August in the Year of Our Lord 1593. In that the hunting of rabbits has been permitted since ancient times, albeit not with the aid of weapons such as spears, bow and arrows, muskets, and the like, I hereby decree that the hunting of rabbits with ferrets be likened to hunting the same with a weapon. From this day forward, therefore, whosoever transgresses this decree shall forfeit his life and liberty."

CHAPTER TEN

A deathly hush descended on the church.

All had grasped at once what the new law signified: From now on, anyone who hunted rabbits with ferrets might end on the gallows!

Hunting without a weapon had been permitted from time immemorial. It would still be permitted — ostensibly. But how else could a person hunt rabbits without a weapon, if not with ferrets? And ferrets had suddenly been declared a weapon.

The Baron had never done such a thing before. Never had he abolished a right that had existed from time immemorial. The villagers did not hunt rabbits themselves; they purchased them from Grim Harry. That enabled them to have some meat on the table, if only on Sundays. But rabbits were not the only point at issue. Could they be sure that the Baron would not soon prohibit the gathering of mushrooms and berries in the forest? That was another traditional right, and not even a baron was entitled to abolish traditional rights. There were few members of the congregation who did not surreptitiously clench their fists.

Everyone looked at Grim Harry. If anyone could muster the courage to question the Baron's dictatorial decree, it was he.

But he sat quite still, staring straight ahead. Although he was seething with rage and indignation inside, he remained outwardly quite unmoved. The Baron was only waiting for him to look up at the gallery. Then everyone would see that he did not accept the new law with due humility but felt as rebellious as they all did. And then the Baron would have a pretext for showing what happened to rebels. So Grim Harry continued to sit there without moving.

I paused to listen. Still nothing to be heard. No snarls, no screams. Nothing stirred.

The castle was utterly silent.

All at once a child's voice broke the hush: "Father, is that the man? Is that the nasty man?"

Grim Harry raised his head and slowly turned to look up at the gallery. He stared at the Baron's daughter — fixed her with his dark, piercing gaze.

"Father! The nasty man frightens me!"

"Show some respect, fellow!" One of the Baron's servants came bustling up the aisle, brandishing a dog whip.

"Leave him be!" called the Baron. And, to Grim Harry: "Do you wish to say something? You have my permission to speak."

Grim Harry hesitated. If he spoke, he would probably be done for. But if he remained silent and was caught hunting rabbits, he would be done for beyond a doubt. He rose to his feet. "With respect, Your Lordship, my ferrets are not weapons, any more than are Your Lordship's hounds."

"Well, I declare!" the Baron said sarcastically. "We have a lawyer in our midst!"

"Rabbits are fair game when hunted without weapons, Your Lordship. That is a traditional right." Grim Harry paused. Then he said, "Traditional rights cannot be abolished."

"My decree contravenes the law — is that what you're saying?"

A breathless hush.

"Yes, Your Lordship, it is."

The morning sun was shining through the window. Back home in the States, I would now have been jogging on my favorite piece of sports equipment, the carousel (an inclined wooden disk that revolves when I run on it). One of Great-Grandmother's many mottoes was "A run at the end of the night makes your daily sleep a delight." Well, I would have to dispense with that pleasure. It was time for me to retire to my nest, but I hesitated.

All was well — or so I dearly hoped. But had my theory about Grim Harry and the ferocious ferrets really turned out to be mistaken? I'd heard nothing while writing. No cries for help, no alarums and excursions. Here in the castle, at least. What about the rabbit warren? Enrico and Caruso hadn't shown their faces all night. I took that to be a good sign.

But it could equally be a bad sign.

a VERY BaD SiGN, iN FaCT.

I clambered out of my cage and started to pace up and down. Then I ran up and down for a bit, but it didn't do much to soothe my nerves. I was just wondering whether to call Sir William and confer with him when the guinea pigs walked in.

"Well?" I said. "Did anything happen?"

"Nothing," said Enrico. "If you're referring to the ferrets."

I DREW a DEEP BREATH.

"If you mean the rabbits, on the other hand . . ." said Caruso.

I held my breath.

". . . our skits were a rip-roaring success."

I breathed out.

"Rabbits," Enrico said eagerly, "make a wonderful audience."

"Every one of our gags went over well," Caruso exulted. "They applauded like mad at the end."

"Really?" I said. "Nibbles, Lucinda, Marmaduke — you mean they were all ecstatic?"

"Caruso," said Enrico, "I do believe His Hamstership begrudges us our success as usual."

"Enrico," said Caruso, "I reckon this is a case for the shrink."

In a flash, Enrico was lying flat on his back. **"HELP ME, DOCTOR!"** he groaned, blowing out his cheeks like a hamster. "I'm green with jealousy!"

"Mhm." Caruso, playing the psychiatrist, sat down beside Enrico and pretended to take notes on a pad. "Feels green with jealousy . . ."

"Well, not exactly green, more — er, pale yellow. Like the innards of a mealworm."

"Mhm." The psychiatrist made another note. "Pale yellow like the innards of a mealworm . . ."

"There's nothing more delicious than a mealworm's innards."

"Mhm," said the psychiatrist, scribbling away. "Nothing more delicious . . ."

"And I never get enough of them. Even when I was a youngster in the pet shop, the others always got more than their share."

"Mhm." Scribble, scribble. "As a youngster, felt underprivileged compared to the other members of his litter . . ."

"I always had this fear that one of them would rob me of my rightful mealworm," Enrico, alias the hamster, said slowly, staring into space. Suddenly, he sat bolt upright. "That's it! At last I know what's wrong with me!" He sprang to his feet. "Hurrah, I'm cured! I don't know how to thank you, doctor."

"No problem. One, two . . ." Caruso made some calculations on his pad. "You owe me precisely four mealworms."

And the guinea pigs flung their paws around each other, squealing with mirth.

Precisely four questions occurred to me as I looked at them: (1) Why did guinea pigs have to exist at all? (2) What made them so sure I wouldn't use my razor-sharp teeth on them? (3) How could I have been sentimental enough, only a minute earlier, to feel concerned for their safety? (4) Should I bite them or not?

"That, my friends," I heard Sir William say, "was one of the most brilliant skits I've ever seen you perform."

That solved my fourth question but posed a fifth: Why did tomcats have to exist?

Sir William came down the stairs. "Freddy," he said, "I know they sometimes crack jokes at your expense."

SOMETIMES? ALWAYS!

"But they add a little spice to our lives, in a manner of speaking. So don't take offense, old boy."

Of course not, Your Lordship. Everyone knows that adding spice to the lives of tomcats and guinea pigs is the sole purpose of my existence.

Enrico and Caruso had gone off to have breakfast with their fans ("Beet leaves — very tasty, but our new friends would welcome something different for a change. You wouldn't, by any chance, have some celery we could take them? No? Pity."). The next to go was Sir William, who tactfully intimated to me that he had "something to do outside" (meaning that he was hankering for a mouse). Soon after that, Mr. John went off to have breakfast with Lord Templeton and the rest of the family.

I had just started to have a snack in my cage — all this talk of breakfast had whetted my appetite — when someone came into the room.

It was a girl.

Annabelle.

Naturally. What other girl could it

128

have been? But for one brief moment I wasn't sure. True, she had auburn hair. Freckles too, but they didn't look so funny anymore. Her face was pale and drawn, and she was staring at me in a strange, wide-eyed way.

"Freddy," she said, "I have to ask you a question." She didn't sound her usual bright and cheerful self. Her voice was strained, as if she found it an effort to speak at all.

I climbed out of my cage, then up the rope ladder to the table. That was when I realized what alarmed me most about Annabelle: her personal aroma. She still smelled of chamomile blossom, but it had now been joined by another scent. It was — I don't know how else to describe it — **THE SMELL OF FEAR.**

I darted over to the laptop and turned it on. Then, deliberately trying to be flip, I typed, *At your service, ma'am.*

Annabelle didn't smile, not one little bit. "I have to ask you a question," she repeated in that curiously strained voice. She paused as if she found it hard to go on. "Have you written any more of 'The Lord of the Ferrets'?"

I stared at her. Had someone seen Grim Harry during the night? If so, who?

"I have to know," Annabelle said fiercely. **"ANSWER ME!"**

Should I admit that I'd broken our agreement? What agreement, though? I'd made no promises. Besides, I could produce good reasons for having written some more.

Yes, I typed, *I worked on the story last night.*

She nodded as if she'd known it already.

I thought it over again, I went on. *It's very unlikely that I conjure up Grim Harry, so to speak. I would have felt completely nuts if I'd abandoned my story.*

Annabelle stared at the screen.

And I was right, I typed. *Or* did *Grim Harry appear to someone last night?*

She went on staring at the screen. Then she started to shake her head, slowly at first, then more and more vehemently. All at once she turned, walked to the door, and left the room without looking back.

Her dragging footsteps resembled those of someone carrying a heavy burden.

Chapter Eleven

The Baron's little daughter went skipping across the meadow with her ball. The meadow lay outside the castle precincts, and she ought really to have been accompanied by an armed guard for her personal protection. Those, at least, were the orders of old Barbara, the Baron's housekeeper. But the little girl had slipped away unobserved, and why not? No one would dare to lay a finger on the daughter of such a powerful nobleman.

So she skipped along the edge of the forest with her plaything, a leather ball stuffed with wool. Exuberantly, she tossed it into the air, and it landed in a thicket.

The Baron's daughter parted the branches to look for it, and there, transfixing her with his keen gaze, stood a tall, swarthy, fierce-faced

figure. It was Grim Harry. She froze as if turned
to stone, unable to move so much as her
little finger.

"Baron's daughter," thundered Grim Harry,
"you are done for!"

She felt her scalp prickle with terror.

"You are done for," he repeated, "unless you
keep silent!"

Despite her terror, the Baron's daughter
thought, Keep silent? About what?

Grim Harry seemed to read her mind. "About my presence here," he said. "If you reveal to a living soul that you saw me, I shall kill your father." He paused. "Your brother too, of course."

Haltingly, the Baron's daughter promised never . . .

"Freddy?"

. . . to tell anyone of their meeting. Whereupon Grim Harry . . .

"Freddy!"

I gave a start. **WHERE WAS I?**

Who was calling me?

I was in my nest, and Enrico and Caruso had been calling me. I'd been asleep. I'd merely been dreaming about the Baron's daughter and Grim Harry. **PHEW!**

"Freddy!" That was Sir William.

I hurriedly emerged from my nest. Sir William and the guinea pigs were sitting just outside my cage. "About time too," said Enrico. "Quick, we've got to go," Caruso insisted.

"Why, what's happened?"

"Something epoch-making, old boy." Sir William grinned. "We're invited to tea. All four of us."

The invitation had been Sebastian's idea.

"I've got something to make up for," he explained when we had all assembled. "I accused Enrico and Caruso of biting me, that's one reason. The other — well, you know what that is."

Was he really sorry for scaring us with that buzzard kite of his? I eyed him suspiciously, but he looked sincere enough. The boy seemed to have changed, somehow.

Tea was served in Sebastian's room, not in the Great Hall as usual. That was because it had been Sebastian's idea, so Lord Templeton assured us, but there was probably an additional reason: We animals weren't considered housebroken enough for the Great Hall. Bertha's wary glances at Enrico and Caruso said it all.

Well-supplied with food, we sat on the table (Bertha had naturally put a blanket under the cloth) with the humans seated around us.

All except for Annabelle, who had remained in her room.

"She isn't feeling well," Lord Templeton explained, anxiously rubbing his bristly chin. "I hope it's nothing serious. I gave her an aspirin just in case."

"It better *not* be anything serious," Bertha growled. "If it is, an aspirin won't help. She's feverish, but she hasn't got a high temperature."

So aNNaBELLE WaS iLL! That was why she'd looked so odd.

We animals hope she'll soon be better, I typed politely (Sebastian had set up his laptop on the table).

"Thank you," said Lord Templeton. "I'll tell her."

Sebastian cleared his throat. "I've been dipping into your books, Freddy. They're brilliant."

135

Well, what do you know!

I'D GAINED ANOTHER READER.

"Enrico and Caruso's poems are especially cool," he went on.

Hmm. Maybe he should stick to nonfiction after all.

Sebastian turned to the guinea pigs. "Could you make up a poem for me?"

What, here and now? What did he want? Something like: "All day long we sing our song/and whistle as we do so./No guinea pigs sing sweeter than/Enrico and Caruso"?

"Of course we could," said Enrico.

I pretended to study Lord Templeton's teacup with interest.

"Freddy?" Sir William prompted me quietly.

Of course we could, I hammered out on the keyboard.

"Great," Sebastian said eagerly. "I can hardly wait."

The boy really had changed, but I wished he hadn't. Now I would have to act as the guinea pigs' typist and write their latest effusion on the screen. They started dictating:

> "Life's like a roller coaster, friends,
> it swoops and soars in turn,
> but when you're feeling gloomy there's
> a lesson you must learn:
> Whatever happens, wear a smile,
> and don't forget to do so.
> Be cheerful like us guinea pigs,
> Enrico and Caruso.

Life isn't just a carousel,
that merely spins around,
nor yet a tread-wheel like the ones
in hamster cages found.
A hamster's tread-wheel drives him nuts,
it's simply bound to do so,
unlike us merry guinea pigs,
Enrico and Caruso.

A host of horrors life can be,
that make your blood run cold.
To face its perils on your own

you must be very bold.
But with a pal it's easier
by far for him and you. So
team up like us guinea pigs,
Enrico and Caruso."

Sebastian, Lord Templeton, Mr. John, and even Bertha applauded enthusiastically. Enrico and Caruso bowed in all directions, and Sir William smiled as proudly as if he were their dad.

At the risk of disappointing the guinea pigs' fans, if any, I'm bound to confess that my own enthusiasm was less than overwhelming — in fact I'd risen on my haunches and my fur was bristling. They'd done it again! The second verse was yet another blatant attack on my hamsterdom! **HOW DARED THOSE LOUTISH GUINEA PIGS!**

"Hey, calm down, Freddy," said Sebastian. "Your books don't mention a tread-wheel. You always use a carousel for jogging, right?"

It was true. I relaxed. As far as I was concerned, Sebastian had changed for the better.

I didn't see Annabelle again that day. She had developed a really high temperature, so Mr. John told us that evening — high enough for Bertha to reerect the cot on which Sebastian had slept the previous night and spend the night in Annabelle's room. As for Sebastian, he went on and on until he was allowed to sleep in his father's room. Bertha, who had to put up another cot in there, was indignant. "Come tomorrow morning," she grumbled, "I won't know who's sleeping where!"

Back in our tower room, Enrico and Caruso insisted on being told several times that their new composition was a knockout ("We simply must know. After all, it's the first time we've appeared live in front of a *human* audience, with the exception of Mr. John!").

140

Sir William, his eyes shining with paternal pride, readily assured them that it was. At last, however, they went off to join the rabbits. To protect them, so they said, but in reality to treat them to a rendition of their latest ditty. What, I wondered, would the rabbits think of us hamsters after hearing it? A song like that wasn't exactly calculated to improve interanimal relations.

What with one thing and another, it was quite a while before I could get down to work that night.

But the time came at last. Seated in front of the laptop, I pressed the start button. As usual, it took a while for the screen to sort itself out. Then I clicked on *My Documents*. To replace the file I'd deleted I had resaved my story (copying *FSC*) under the file name *The Lord of the Ferrets*. I tried to access it.

NO DICE.

Instead, a window appeared, and in the window were the words *File not found.*

Hmm. I'd probably saved it elsewhere by mistake. Stranger things had happened before now. But where was it? I instituted a general search, but the same message appeared: *File not found.*

I stared at the screen. My story wasn't there anymore! IT MUST HAVE BEEN DELETE!

Had I inadvertently erased it? Most unlikely. What about Mr. John? That was a possibility. He'd made some notes on the laptop that afternoon. Whatever the truth, my story had disappeared, just like that.

But there was still *FSC (Freddy's Secret Copy)*. I had also updated that last night. I could only pray that it hadn't been deleted too.

I clicked my way to where the file name *FSC* had to be, and there it was.

I retrieved it and resaved it again as *The Lord of the Ferrets.*

The warren was more extensive than Grim Harry had thought. He must have overlooked several exit tunnels, because nearly all the rabbits had escaped. Only three had become entangled in his nets, and they were wretchedly small. It would be pointless to flush this warren out again. Grim Harry debated whether to go in search of another, but the weather was as sultry as it had been for several afternoons past, and a storm was brewing.

Grim Harry shouldered the box containing the ferrets, his nets, and his carrying pole with the rabbits dangling from it.

Which homeward route should he take?

He could safely take the route across the fields. The villagers were welcome to see that his bag was meager, and besides, he would be less likely to run into the Baron there. The Baron traversed his fields less often than his forest. Above all, Grim Harry would sight him from afar and be able to hide.

Why hide?

He had no reason to hide from the Baron. On Sunday he had told him to his face that the new law was unjust, and the Baron had listened without ordering his arrest. His Lordship was no fool. He had looked into the villagers' faces and quickly grasped that his new decree went too far — in fact, Grim Harry considered it his duty to make this abundantly clear.

He resolved to take the track through the forest.

He reached the giant beech that had been struck by lightning the previous year without encountering the Baron or any of his gamekeepers, but he was still less than halfway home. He walked on tensely. Although he thought he knew what he was doing, he wasn't entirely sure. What if the Baron had him arrested after all?

Grim Harry reached his cottage on the edge of the forest without meeting a soul

Relieved, he crossed the little kitchen garden behind the cottage, vaguely surprised that his approach hadn't startled the wood pigeons that made a habit of raiding his seed beds, and opened the door.

They were waiting for him.

Grim Harry's cottage was full of the Baron's armed retainers.

He hadn't the slightest chance of escaping . . .

How should the story continue? I stared at the screen, lost in thought. Should I now describe Grim Harry's capture, or would it be better to skip that and go straight on to describe how the Baron . . .

I caught a movement out of the corner of my eye.

My head jerked around.

And there they were.

THE FEROCIOUS FERRETS!

CHAPTER TWELVE

THE HUGE CREATURES STOOD poised on the edge of
the table, rearing up on their haunches with their fur shim-
mering in the greenish glow from the laptop's screen.
Their mouths were wide open, and their needle-sharp
teeth stood out white against the dark recesses of their
throats.

They were utterly silent.

Not a snarl could be heard, and the bells on their
collars made no sound.

Still motionless but ready to pounce, they gazed at
me through slitted eyes.

I myself had reared up in terror, fur bristling madly,
cheek pouches inflated, and teeth bared. It was a
hamster's instinctive threat posture, but it naturally failed
to impress those two gigantic predators.

Sir William! If anyone was a match for them, he was.
"Sir William!" I called in Interanimal.

Nothing stirred upstairs in Mr. John's room.

"Sir William! Help!"

Silence.

"**HELP!!!**"

Sir William was obviously sound asleep. The ferrets' hideous faces, with their slit eyes and gaping jaws, had twisted into a grimace of contempt.

I was frozen, paralyzed with fear, but my brain was still functioning. Feverishly, I debated what to do.

I already knew, because it was the only thing that could still save me.

Except that the ferrets would pounce the instant I moved. I would have only a fraction of a second to spare. A tiny fraction.

I sat absolutely still — I even had my whiskers under control. With supreme concentration, I worked out what to do and in what order. Above all, I formed a mental picture of where everything was. I programmed my movements, so to speak. Each of them had to work the first time and none must fail, because I wouldn't get a second chance.

Careful not to move, I drew a deep breath.

AND TOOK THE PLUNGE.

Quick as a flash, I pressed the keys I had to press, then flattened myself on the table in front of the keyboard.

Here they came.

They performed such a prodigious leap, they literally flew at me.

I followed their progress through the air as if watching a slow-motion replay. But why wasn't my plan working?

Go on! Now! *Now*, or it would be too late. . . .

And then it happened: The ferrets became blurred.

They became blurred as I watched, turned transparent, and vanished just as they were about to pounce on me.

I had done it.

I'd managed to close the program and exit my story.

I'd succeeded in banishing the ferrets.

For a while I simply lay flat on my tummy in front of the keyboard. Having summoned up all the presence of mind and concentration of which a golden hamster is capable (just between you and me, even I felt surprised by the extent of my powers), I was utterly exhausted.

But why had the ferrets taken so long to vanish, almost as if they were reluctant to do so? They naturally hadn't wanted to return to the world of the Undead, but it had seemed to me that they'd been counting on *not* having to vanish. **OR Had I ONLY iMAGiNED THAT?**

I resolved not to think about it anymore. First I had to recuperate.

I'd just done so, more or less, when there was a knock on the door of our tower room. Whoever it was knocked again, more loudly, until Mr. John turned on the light and came hurrying downstairs in his bathrobe. He opened the door.

"Good heavens," he exclaimed, "what's the matter?"

Everyone was there: Lord Templeton, Sebastian, Annabelle, and Bertha.

"We'd like a word with you right away," Lord Templeton said grimly, with a look on his face that boded no good. "It's about that hamster of yours."

"About Freddy? Now, at this hour of the night?"

Mr. John raised his eyebrows. "All right, come in," he said. "Please have a seat," he added, but only Bertha sat down. She gave me a hostile glare, and Annabelle, who had lingered just inside the door, looked daggers at me with her eyes. Lord Templeton and Sebastian stood side by side in the middle of the room.

I can't pretend I felt particularly comfortable at that moment.

"I insist that you put a stop to your hamster's activities," Lord Templeton said indignantly to Mr. John. "And I —"

"Sorry to interrupt," Mr. John cut in, "but may I know to which of Freddy's activities you're referring?"

"You may." Lord Templeton drew a deep breath. "But first I must tell you something: Only half an hour ago, I'd have sent for a straitjacket if anyone had predicted . . ." He shook his head. All at once, it became clear that his anger was born of fear. "I mean, in my own bedroom . . ." He broke off again.

"That giant appeared again," said Sebastian.

"I'LL SAY HE DID!" said Lord Templeton. "He was flesh and blood — he couldn't possibly have been a dream, especially since Sebastian saw him too."

"And this time he spoke," Sebastian put in.

"Really?"

"Yes," said Lord Templeton, "except that he was hard to follow. He spoke a very old-fashioned kind of English, but I definitely caught the words 'death' and 'kill.' And they were clearly meant for me and Sebastian." He looked at Mr. John. "I'm sure you must find this quite incredible, but I swear it's what happened."

"Why shouldn't I believe you?" Mr. John said gravely. "Incredible things happen more often than we think. There's only one point that puzzles me," he went on. "What does Freddy have to do with this apparition?"

Before her father could reply, Annabelle said brusquely, "Freddy! Have you been working on your story again?"

I could simply have nodded, but that might have looked as if I felt to blame in some way. *Yes,* I typed on the keyboard. *But there's no real proof of our theory.*

"What theory?" asked Mr. John.

"That Freddy conjures up Grim Harry and his ferrets whenever he works on his story," said Annabelle. "PERSONALLY, I THINK IT'S A FACT And she went on to describe our deliberations of the day before. The lucid way in which she did so conveyed that her temperature had gone down. "And that," she concluded, "is why Freddy mustn't write any more of his story, not under any circumstances."

"Hmm." Mr. John plucked at his eyebrow.

Annabelle's account had been accurate and pretty detailed. The one thing she'd failed to mention was that I'd done some more writing the previous night as well, and that neither Grim Harry nor his ferrets had appeared that time.

I was about to remind her of this when Mr. John said

suddenly, "Freddy, you wouldn't by any chance have that case from 1593 on file, would you?"

I certainly would, I typed. *I copied it out carefully. After all, my story's based on it.*

"QU**I**TE SO," said Mr. John. "Please show it to us." And, to Lord Templeton: "It comes from a collection of legal judgments published in the eighteenth century. I think it's historically accurate."

I retrieved the relevant file:

In a small barony in the West Country, a certain poacher was subjected to harsher punishment than anyone could remember. The said poacher, whom folk called Grim Harry on account of his sinister cast of feature, had killed three rabbits on the Baron's land with the aid of two ferrets. On the 30th day of August, Anno Domini 1593, having been apprehended and imprisoned, he was sentenced by the Baron, sitting in judgment, to die on the gallows as a dire example to others. The ferrets, which were exceptionally large, had previously, being guilty of the same offense as Grim Harry, been drowned without mercy.

"I'm wondering," said Mr. John, "whether there may be some connection between the barony mentioned in this judgment and Templeton Castle." He broke off. "Why, Lord Templeton, what's the matter?"

Lord Templeton was staring at the screen wide-eyed. At length he ran a hand over his eyes and shook his head. "This is weird," he muttered. He read the passage through once more.

Then he drew a deep breath and said, "There certainly is a connection. The baron who sentenced that poacher to death in 1593 was an ancestor of mine."

Silence fell. Lord Templeton's announcement took time to sink in. Everyone stared at him, then at the screen, then at him again.

"I must have been around Sebastian's age," he went on, "when my father read me that very passage out of a big book bound in pigskin. 'That baron,' he told me, 'was an ancestor of ours, my boy.'"

"But why did you never tell us about it?" Annabelle asked.

"Because the story completely slipped my mind. I've never given it a thought in all these years."

157

"What about the book?" Sebastian asked. "The one with the pigskin cover? Does it still exist?"

"I think so," said Lord Templeton. "It should be in the library, with all the other books about our family. *The Chronicle of the Barony of Templeton*, for instance."

"The what?"

"*The Chronicle of the Barony of Templeton*. A history of this place, written long ago by the parish parson." Lord Templeton looked back at the screen. "To think I'd forgotten all about the story. . . . Maybe it was because an ancestor like that is hardly a source of pride."

"He certainly wasn't softhearted," said Bertha. "Hanging a man for the sake of three rabbits? Charming! You've got to look at it from the poacher's point of view. No wonder his ghost comes walking through the walls."

"a GHOST?" said Lord Templeton. "Is that what you think he is?"

"Can you think of another word for what you saw?"

Lord Templeton nodded. "Yes, I can. Grim Harry

isn't a ghost, **HE'S ONE OF THE UNDEAD.**
When he appears he's really here — he's come here from
the world of the Undead. What's more, I'm convinced he
can kill us if he chooses." Lord Templeton paused. Then
he said, "That's why there's only one answer." He looked
at me. "You must stop writing, Freddy."

NOT SO FAST, YOUR LORDSHIP!

It was still only a theory. There was no real proof that my
writing conjured up Grim Harry and his ferrets.

"Freddy," said Mr. John. "There's no real proof, is
there?"

I shook my head.

"But there's just a chance, and it can't be ignored.
Right?"

Right, I typed reluctantly.

"So there's just a chance that someone will get killed.
Right?"

Right, I typed. And, after a pause: *Okay, I'll abandon my
story. I'll delete it.*

"Promise?"

Cross my heart, Mr. John.

Annabelle said, "Why not do it right away?"

"Yes, why not?" said Lord Templeton. "For safety's sake."

Everyone looked at me expectantly, Mr. John included. It was obvious they all thought me capable of breaking my word. I wondered whether to take offense, but decided that I couldn't care less what they thought of me. Just to punish them, I naturally wouldn't breathe a word about *FSC (Freddy's Secret Copy)*. That was my business, and I would attend to it later. So I clicked my way to *The Lord of the Ferrets* and pressed the delete key.

"Fine," said Bertha, "so that's the end of Mr. Undead." She got up. "With a bit of luck, our nights won't be so lively in the future."

I looked over at Annabelle.

She was standing in the doorway, arms folded, staring at me in silence with a forbidding frown.

CHaPTER THIRTEEN

SHOULD I REALLY DELETE *Freddy's Secret Copy?*
I wanted to get it over with as soon as I was alone again. That would dispose of my story once and for all, and I could start on another with my brain spring-cleaned, so to speak.

But when I'd highlighted file name *FSC* and was about to press the delete key, **I COULDN'T DO IT.**

I had written hundreds and hundreds of words. I'd not only typed them out but marshaled them into sentences that embodied ideas and told a story. The laptop was a store chamber in which I'd amassed a treasure. Was I now to destroy that treasure? It was asking too much of me. A hamster simply cannot bring himself to destroy his stores. I had no intention of writing any more of my story — that I swear — but I wanted to keep it. For the moment, at least.

I turned off the laptop, climbed down my rope ladder, and curled up in my nest.

Sir William woke me late that afternoon.

"I gather you deleted your story last night," he said as I crawled out of my nest. "You must be very upset, I imagine."

That, Sir William, earns you a gold medal for acute sensitivity.

"However, old boy, you mustn't be too depressed. You could even take the opportunity to give up writing altogether. It would eliminate the excessive and unnatural strain on your gray matter."

You've just earned another

gold medal, Sir William, this time for badly under-estimating a hamster's mental capacity.

"Be that as it may, Freddy, we've received an invitation."

"**REALLY?** From whom?"

"Enrico and Caruso — they're putting on a show for the rabbits. I think we should accept. I'm sure you'd benefit from a little light entertainment. For my part, I'd welcome some more of their uproariously amusing skits."

Sir William knows a great deal about life. He's what you'd call a wise old tomcat, but logic isn't his forte.

Why writing stories should harm a hamster's brain, whereas making up skits leaves a guinea pig's brain unaffected, is a secret known only to himself.

Perhaps even Sir William suspects that it doesn't strain the intellect too much to knock out simple skits with a single theme, namely, bugging Freddy.

"I accept their invitation," I said, "but only on one condition: **NO JOKES AT MY EXPEN-**

"I'll convey your request to Enrico and Caruso. All the same, old boy," Sir William said with a rueful shake of the head, "I find it most regrettable that you hamsters so obviously lack the ability to laugh at yourselves."

Another gold medal, this time awarded to myself for self-control while listening to a ludicrous remark.

The show took place beneath the bramble thicket behind the barn, where a relatively large open space formed a kind of circus ring to which the artistes could gain access via a single rabbit hole in the center.

The audience, which had already assembled, was much bigger than I'd expected. Some fifty rabbits were chatting together as they waited with ears expectantly pricked for the show to begin. To a conceited couple like Enrico and Caruso, such an exceptionally large colony of rabbits must have seemed like a gift from the gods. I could now understand, if only vaguely, why they'd volunteered to guard the warren at the risk of being bitten by the ferrets.

Sir William and I were conducted to our seats in a sort of box enclosed by bramble shoots.

Just then everyone fell silent: Marmaduke had emerged from the artistes' entrance. He drew himself up with an air of great self-importance. "Does and bucks! Honored guests!" he cried, raising his forepaws. "Welcome to . . . the show of shows! It will be my pleasure and privilege to guide you through this afternoon's program. And now," he cried, pointing to the artistes' entrance, "here they come! Give a big welcome to those celebrated guinea pigs: ENRICO AND CARUSO!" So saying, he disappeared down the hole.

And Enrico and Caruso emerged.

A wild ovation . . . I had often seen the expression on paper but had never really known what it meant. Now I knew: A wild ovation meant that the ground shook and

the air vibrated because fifty rabbits were drumming on the ground with their hind legs.

Enrico and Caruso bowed in all directions for a while, and the deafening din continued. Then they raised their forepaws and silence fell at once.

"**THANK YOU, FRIENDS!**" said Enrico. "We're very touched — indeed, overwhelmed, aren't we, Caruso?"

"You can say that again, Enrico. Shouldn't we . . ." Caruso whispered something in Enrico's ear.

Enrico shook his head. "My partner," he announced, "was wondering whether we should go straight into our song."

"We composed it especially for you," said Caruso. "But I agree, we'd better save it for the end."

"So first we've got a different treat in store." They bowed again and dove down the hole.

Marmaduke reappeared. He rose on his haunches as before (a position as normal for a rabbit as it is for the likes of me), but then he began to pace majestically up and down on his hind legs. He looked so ridiculous, the rabbits around us started to titter. Marmaduke was too busy putting on airs to notice.

"Esteemed members of the audience," he boomed, "I now have the pleasure" — Enrico and Caruso emerged from the rabbit hole, each painted like a red-nosed clown — "in announcing the next act." Marmaduke hadn't seen them. They sneaked up behind him, rose on their hind paws, and mimicked his majestic gait. The rabbits doubled up with suppressed laughter.

169

"You will now see . . ." Marmaduke turned around, but Enrico and Caruso dodged behind him so nimbly that he failed to spot them. Many of the rabbits stifled their laughter by biting their paws. "You will now see the incredible . . . NÌBBLES!"

Marmaduke threw up his forepaws. Behind him, keeping time with him perfectly, the two clowns did likewise. The rabbits, who couldn't contain themselves any longer, roared with laughter.

Marmaduke looked around him in bewilderment, but Enrico and Caruso had already vanished down the hole. "Thank you," he said with a smile, bowing. "You're all very kind."

I was enjoying myself immensely. Perhaps because Enrico and Caruso really hadn't cracked any jokes at my expense, but more probably because they hadn't presented any skits at all, and they were genuinely good at playing the clown.

If it hadn't been for them, for instance, Nibbles's act would have been instantly forgettable. True, he performed some incredible aerial leaps, on one occasion attaining such an altitude that he seemed in danger of becoming lodged in the brambles overhead. What transformed this into a circus act, however, was the presence of the clowns. While Nibbles was in the air, Enrico and Caruso scampered after him with outstretched paws, ready to catch him — only to dart aside when he came down. Poor Nibbles, who had probably been counting on a soft landing, hit the ground with a thud every time.

To be honest, the more often I saw this, the funnier I found it.

Then there was Lucinda's song. Someone, possibly Lucinda herself, had come up with the idea that she should sing it atop a three-storied pyramid of buck rabbits. When nine of them had laboriously formed this pyramid (not an overly impressive acrobatic feat), Lucinda stationed herself at the very top. To prevent her from falling, the two rabbits immediately beneath her clung tightly to her hind legs.

Lucinda proceeded to sing. "CELERY, CELERY, CELERY, CELER she warbled. "I dream of celery all day long. Why, oh why can I never get any . . ." Abruptly, she broke off and looked down. Her eyes widened.

The clowns came strolling up, and each of them (heavens knows where they'd gotten hold of the stuff) was nibbling a stick of celery.

"Let me down!" Lucinda hissed to her two supports, but they hesitated. Having put a lot of work into forming the pyramid, they

expected her to complete her act. "Let me down this minute!" Lucinda hissed again, trying to free her hind legs. She struggled even harder, the pyramid started to sway, tottered more and more perilously, and then (the clowns had long since made themselves scarce, of course) all ten rabbits collapsed in a heap. If golden hamsters could weep with laughter, I would have shed a tear or two.

The next act was another musical number: A trio of drummers beat out "Augustus Thumper's Tattoo." Augustus Thumper (so we were informed by a doe in the next box) had lived in very ancient times. He could sprint incredibly fast, and his unrivaled ability to zigzag when pursued by hounds had made him something of a folk hero. Few rabbit festivities were complete without an enthusiastic rendition of this drumroll in his honor.

Hmm. To a non-rabbit, the din made by those three drummers was not productive of enthusiasm — in fact, its effect could have been described as sending one to sleep. It would take all the clowns' artistry to rescue this act. I couldn't wait to see what Enrico and Caruso had concocted. But where were they?

I looked at the artistes' entrance. Nothing.

The drumming went on and on and on. If something didn't happen soon, I really would go to sleep.

But here they came.

Like a pair of rockets, Enrico and Caruso shot out of the central rabbit hole so fast, they sailed through the air and landed with two dull thuds.

Whoops of delight went up from the rabbits around us. That was the sort of entrance they enjoyed! Startled, the trio of drummers stopped drumming. Enrico and Caruso must naturally have been counting on this (as clowns, they genuinely knew their stuff).

They scrambled to their feet and pointed to the artistes' entrance with every sign of terror.

"Th-there!" Enrico stammered, seemingly scared to death.

"L-look!" Caruso stuttered, as if he'd just encountered a monster.

The rabbits laughed so hard, their ears flapped.

How much would you bet that Marmaduke would appear next, and once again without a clue what the game was?

Sure enough, out of the hole he shot. What a scream! And he was in disguise too!

He drew himself up to his full height. But . . . how tall he looked — absolutely huge!

Then a second, equally huge figure shot out of the hole. . . . It was . . .

Like blocks of ice, the rabbits froze with terror.

IT WAS THE FERRETS.

Chapter Fourteen

IT WAS THE FEROCIOUS FERRETS.

They reared up on their haunches, snarling mouths wide open.

The little bells on their collars jangled shrilly.

The rabbits sat rooted to the spot.

The ferrets looked around, taking stock of the situation. Their very first leap into the midst of that close-packed audience would bring them rich pickings. Then would come what ferrets enjoyed most of all: a rabbit hunt.

They prepared to pounce.

At that moment, a black shape darted into view.

IT WAS SIR WILLIAM.

One mighty leap took him from the shelter of our box and out into the open. He faced the ferrets, poised to launch himself at them.

I had never seen him in his attack mode before. His tail lashed the air, the fur on his neck and back bristled like a flue brush, his ears were flattened, and his gaping mouth, with its enormous fangs, emitted such a menacing, piercing, swelling growl that my own fur involuntarily stood on end.

The ferrets, bracing themselves on their hind legs, bared their teeth and snarled back. They were smaller than Sir William, but not much. Above all, there were two of them.

Sir William and the ferrets stood confronting one another.

Suddenly, Sir William sprang at them. Simultaneously, as if that had brought them to life again, the rabbits took off. They stampeded in all directions, each trying to dive down the nearest hole. In the chaos that broke out all around me I caught a glimpse of Enrico and Caruso fleeing in terror. Then I saw that Sir William had failed to catch either of the ferrets.

They had leaped aside. Just as he turned to face the ferret on his right, the other one sprang at him and sank its teeth into his flank. Sir William turned his head and tried to bite it, but its partner sprang at him too and got a grip on his throat. Sir William growled madly and shook himself.

But the ferrets would not let go. On the contrary, the more wildly Sir William shook himself, the firmer their grip seemed to become. It would not be long before their yellowish snouts were stained with his blood.

And then, with a mighty jerk of the head, Sir William dislodged the ferret hanging on to his throat and sent it

flying. He snapped, once, twice, at the creature biting his flank and managed to drive his teeth into its back. But no blood came, and it continued to hang on tight. Then the other one sprang at him once more and caught hold of one of his hind legs.

Sir William turned and snapped at the beasts again and again, but to no avail. I could clearly detect that his movements were getting slower.

Two ferrets were more than a match for him.

Sir William was losing the battle.

Gripping him firmly in their teeth, the ferrets would simply wait until his strength ran out.

And then . . .

THEN iT HAPPENED.

Almost imperceptibly at first, then ever faster, the ferrets turned transparent. They paled before my eyes. Their jaws too seemed to become weaker, because Sir William suddenly quieted and stood waiting.

At last they disappeared.

I darted over to Sir William. "Are you badly hurt?"

"What injuries are you referring to, old boy?" He gave me a wry smile. "If you mean my pride — the pride of a tomcat hoping to win a fight — yes, I have to admit that my pride is hurt. As for my physical injuries, they're only minor." He shook his hind leg. "It'll soon be better, my friend. What really worries me," he went on, "is something else."

"You mean the fact that the beasts appeared even though I hadn't done any writing?"

"Precisely. I suggest we find out if anything has happened back at the castle." He lowered his head. "JUMP ON."

※ ※ ※

Something *had* happened at the castle.

When Sir William and I entered the Great Hall, Lord Templeton and his family had assembled there with Mr. John. Bertha was sitting in an armchair with the others clustered around her. A first-aid kit was lying on the table, and her thumb was thickly bandaged. Her cheeks were pale, and she was actually trembling a little.

"Shall I get you a brandy?" Annabelle asked.

Bertha shook her head. "Take to drink because of Mr. Undead? Not me!"

Annabelle laughed. She had changed since last night. She seemed genuinely relaxed, and she smelled of pure chamomile blossom again. The scent of fear had gone.

"Well, how did it happen?" asked Lord Templeton.

"It was like this," Bertha explained. "I was sitting at the kitchen table, slicing some tomatoes for supper, when I suddenly noticed something. I got this sensation you get when someone's watching you."

"What's it like?" asked Sebastian.

"You feel it, that's all. Anyway, I got this sensation and

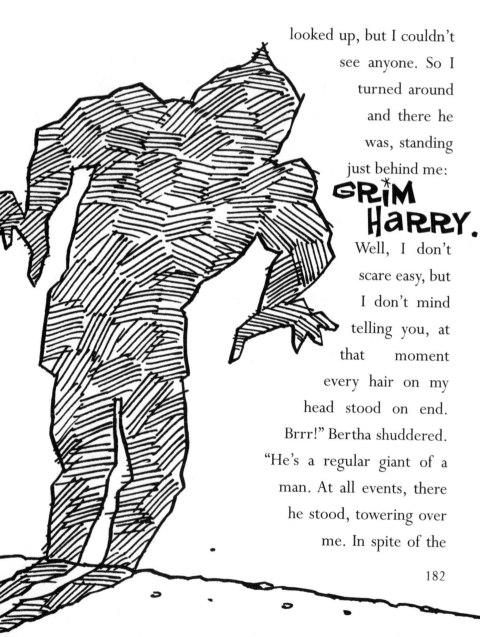

looked up, but I couldn't see anyone. So I turned around and there he was, standing just behind me: **GRIM HARRY.**

Well, I don't scare easy, but I don't mind telling you, at that moment every hair on my head stood on end. Brrr!" Bertha shuddered. "He's a regular giant of a man. At all events, there he stood, towering over me. In spite of the

182

shock he'd given me, I noticed that his boots were caked with mud. The clothes he wears are old-fashioned-looking and pretty dirty. Very rough and ready too. Every seam crooked and no two buttonholes the same. It's hardly surprising, I suppose. There weren't any sewing machines in those days. Everything had to be sewn by hand, and —"

"That's all very interesting," Lord Templeton broke in, "but what happened next?"

"He stood staring down at me, and I stared back. I remember thinking he didn't look the picture of health, to say the least. His face was grayish-green, like rotten meat. What *he* was thinking I've no idea, but he certainly had something in mind, judging by the way he looked at me. Eyes like skewers, he had — they seemed to go right through me." Bertha paused. "Well, and then it happened."

"What happened?"

"This." Bertha raised her bandaged thumb. "I don't know what possessed me — it sounds so stupid — but I started slicing my tomatoes again. The knife slipped and I cut my thumb." She clicked her tongue.

"And then?"

"Then he disappeared. Not all at once, but little by little. I watched him turning more and more transparent until he vanished."

"Did he speak at all?" asked Lord Templeton.

"No, he was silent as the grave." Bertha thought for a moment. "I wonder what he wanted." She shrugged. "Perhaps he simply wanted to see who's living in the castle these days."

"What he wanted isn't so important," said Mr. John. "What's far *more* important is how he managed to appear. Freddy," he went on (Sir William, with me on his back, had stationed himself where everyone could see us), "did you start to rewrite your story?"

I stiffened and was about to shake my head when Annabelle said, very firmly, "No, he didn't."

HUH? What made her so sure?

Annabelle turned to me. "Have the ferrets appeared again too?" she asked. "Outside, where the rabbits live?"

I nodded vigorously, then indicated Sir William.

Annabelle came over to us. "Goodness!" she exclaimed. "**HE'S HURT!** Was it the ferrets?"

I nodded again. Mr. John also came over and examined Sir William. "Poor old fellow," he said. "Never mind, I'll bet you showed them a thing or two, eh?"

I confirmed this with another vigorous nod.

"We must take him to the vet right away!" Annabelle cried anxiously.

"No." Mr. John shook his head. "He doesn't need any stitches. These wounds will heal better if we let Sir William tend them himself. Right, old fellow?"

Sir William uttered a little mew.

Lord Templeton rubbed his bristly gray chin. "So the Undead can now appear without being summoned by Freddy."

"Sorry to disagree," said Mr. John, "but I don't think Freddy ever summoned them." He plucked at his eyebrow. "Grim Harry wants to escape from the world of the Undead, complete with his ferrets. Perhaps he's been trying to do so for centuries, but without success. He needed an opening of some kind, and Freddy's story supplied it."

"But why doesn't he need it anymore?" Annabelle asked. "The story, I mean?"

"I suspect his visits to us have strengthened him, rather like the effect of training on an athlete." Mr. John smiled faintly, only to turn serious again. "But he's still not strong enough to stay for very long."

"If he goes on like this he soon will be," said Bertha. "And then, goodness help us."

"But what can he actually do to us?" Annabelle asked. "He may have frightened Great-Aunt Agatha to death, but he can't do that to us, not anymore. I mean, everyone in the family has seen Grim Harry now. . . ." She paused, then added quickly, "Except me. Anyway," she went on, "we now know the monster for what he is. We aren't going to die of fright if we . . . **EEK!**"

THE DOOR OF THE GREAT HALL
HAD BURST OPEN
WITH A THUNDEROUS CRASH.

Chapter Fifteen

THE MASSIVE DOOR CRASHED against the wall, then swung back and slammed shut.

It was the wind. A gale had sprung up outside, as it so often had in the past few days. All the doors were left ajar to allow us animals to come and go.

We were all terribly startled, not just Annabelle. Sebastian was clinging to his father's arm, and Bertha had jumped up with her hands clasped to her bosom.

"Well," she said, breathing heavily, "we may not be frightened, but our nerves are pretty shaky."

"Speaking of nerves," Mr. John said to Annabelle, "you mustn't forget how long ago Grim Harry lived. In those days people were beheaded, burned at the stake — even hung, drawn, and quartered. They were also tortured. People of today couldn't bear to watch such things. If Grim Harry were capable of showing us scenes like that, we might well die of fright."

Annabelle stared at him wide-eyed. She opened her mouth to speak but shut it again. After a while she said, "And besides, who's to say he can't do anything to us with his own hands?"

'VE GOT IT!" Bertha exclaimed. "Of course! *That* was the reason."

"What was?" asked Lord Templeton. "And for what?"

"Well, for why Grim Harry turned up. I was wondering why he did, and now I think I know." Bertha shook her head. "I'm a bit slow sometimes."

"Would it be asking too much of you," said Lord Templeton, "to share your sudden flash of inspiration with us?"

"Very well, Your Lordship." Bertha grinned. "Grim Harry came to show us he can do more than scare us. He can actually hurt us."

Mr. John frowned. "You mean he *made* you cut yourself?"

"Yes. He was telling us: Look, folks, I can actually draw blood."

189

"Well," said Mr. John, "that sounds ominous."

"It does indeed." Lord Templeton rubbed his stubbly chin again. "So the question arises: How do we protect ourselves from this monster?"

"How about calling the police?" asked Mr. John. "We ought at least to consider the possibility. Just to be on the safe side," he added quickly.

"If I called them and reported that Templeton Castle was being haunted by a sixteenth-century poacher and two ferrets, they'd laugh themselves sick."

Mr. John nodded. "I see what you mean."

"Well," Lord Templeton went on, "he mustn't catch us on our own." He surveyed the Great Hall. "We'll all have to spend the night in here. Do we have enough camp beds, Bertha?" ("Camp bed," I assumed, was the English term for "cot.")

"Plenty, but may Grim Harry take me if I put them up on my own. You two," she told Annabelle and Sebastian, "can give me a hand."

"One for me too, please," said Mr. John.

"Of course." Bertha turned to go. "And only yesterday I was wondering who would be sleeping where." She stomped off. "Everyone bedded down in the Great Hall! Who would have thought it!"

While the sleeping arrangements were being attended to, Sir William and I (perched on his neck) made our way back to the warren. We naturally had to warn the rabbits and Enrico

and Caruso that the ferrets might reappear at any
moment — and that they would probably take up
permanent residence in our world.

"What then?" I asked. "I mean, how on earth can we
protect the rabbits?"

"Why ask *me* that, old boy? You're only rubbing salt
into my wounds."

"I'm sorry, Sir William," I told him, and I meant it. My
question was not only tactless but superfluous. There was
no way we could protect the rabbits. Big though it was,
their colony would probably be extinct before long.

The gale was still blowing, but it seemed to be
subsiding. Just as we were crossing the courtyard, Enrico
and Caruso came scuttling toward us.

I find it rather embarrassing to recount what happened next. I mean, everyone knows that guinea pigs tend to be dense. But I myself? And Sir William?

Anyway, Enrico cried, "You're just in time for the ceremony!"

"**EREMONY?**" said Sir William. "What ceremony?"

"Nibbles, Lucinda, and Marmaduke are waiting outside the gate. They've come to convey their colony's gratitude to you."

"For saving them from the ferrets," Caruso amplified.

Sir William shook his head. "I didn't save them."

"Er, we know that, Sir William." Enrico was looking sheepish for some reason. "The ferrets simply evaporated. We both saw it, of course."

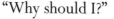

"But the rabbits didn't. They think you drove them away with your teeth and claws." Caruso was also looking sheepish. "Could you possibly stick to that version, Sir William? That you were responsible for getting rid of them, I mean?"

"Why should I?"

Enrico was positively squirming with embarrassment now. "Because, er, we bragged about you a little."

"More than a little, maybe," said Caruso. Suddenly, he blurted out, "We really went to town on the story."

"And the rabbits applauded. We basked in your reflected glory, so to speak."

"You expect me to lie for you?" Sir William shook his head again. "Certainly not. Pride comes before a fall, as my late father used to say. You can atone for your dishonesty by telling them the truth."

We went over to the gateway, where Lucinda, Nibbles, and Marmaduke were waiting. Enrico and Caruso hid behind Sir William. It must have been terribly embarrassing for them to be unmasked as show-offs.

Marmaduke drew himself up to his full height. "Esteemed Sir William!" Having cleared his throat self-importantly, he declaimed:

*"Sir William's fame throughout the world
resounds. A most heroic sight,*

with flashing teeth and claws unsheathed
those ferrets he did put to flight.
Quite heedless of his wounds he —"

"**STOP, THAT'S ENOUGH!**" cried Sir
William. "You're mistaken." He stepped aside and
pointed to Enrico and Caruso, who had flattened
themselves like fireside rugs. "Mistaken like our two
friends here," he went on. "They're also
under the impression that I
drove the ferrets away."
Enrico and Caruso raised
their heads and looked
at each other. They
obviously couldn't
believe their
luck. Being
bighearted
(in this case a
bit too bighearted,

if you ask me), Sir William had refrained from giving them away.

"It was none of my doing that the ferrets disappeared," said Sir William. "Freddy will now fill you in on the background to this affair."

I slid off Sir William's back and took up my position at a considerable distance from him. I wanted to show the rabbits that the said affair had nothing to do (at least initially) with Sir William, their celebrated feline hero, let alone with Enrico and Caruso, their favorite entertainers. **I, FREDDY,** the diminutive but sharp-witted hamster, was the principal character in this drama.

"Well," I said, "it all began with an ancient book." I described how I had come across the case of Grim Harry, and how I had started to write a story based on it. In response to a question from Lucinda, I told the rabbits how I had learned to read and write, what a computer was, and that I was now regarded as an author of considerable repute. Next, I described what had happened at Templeton Castle since our arrival. I presented a detailed account of the connection between my story and the appearance of the Undead, who had lately managed to materialize without my writing a word. "They may return at any moment," I concluded, "and then they may stay here forever."

A lengthy silence fell.

Lucinda and Nibbles were evidently pondering what they had heard. Marmaduke too seemed to be thinking hard, because he was staring into space and rhythmically tapping his nose with one paw. After a while he looked around and announced the result of his cogitations: "If the creatures stayed here forever, it would mean we'd have to live with them in the future, wouldn't it?"

"L-live with th-them?" Nibbles performed a diagonal leap. **WHAT DO YOU MEAN, LIVE TH THEM? THEY'D MASSACRE US!"**

"There must be some defense against them," said Lucinda.

"I'm afraid not, my dear." Sir William shook his head. "*I'm* certainly no match for them."

"I doubt if even humans could harm them," I put in. "It's true they do their dirty work in our world, but they're **UNDEAD.** They belong in a different world."

Another long silence.

Marmaduke continued to stare into space and tap his nose. "If they belong in their own world, they've no business in ours, correct?"

Nobody commented on this statement of the obvious.

Marmaduke went on tapping his nose. Suddenly, he turned to me and said, "You must send them back to *their* world!"

"Oh, sure," I said. He was beginning to get on my nerves. "The next time Grim Harry and his ferrets appear, I'll simply tell them, 'You've no business here, guys, so kindly get lost and never show your faces around here again.'"

"Of course you won't *tell* them that. You must *write* it."

"Sure." I was getting mad. "I'll drop them a postcard — that'll really impress them."

"MY DEAR SIR!" Marmaduke looked down his nose at me. "You're being a trifle slow on the uptake. You've been writing this story — what was it called again?"

" 'The Lord of the Ferrets,' " I said, grinding my teeth. Marmaduke was becoming a genuine challenge to my self-control.

"Ah yes, 'The Lord of the Ferrets,' " he said. "So you've been working on this story, correct?"

"Correct." Cool it, Freddy. Don't let this knucklehead

drive you up the wall — wither him with icy contempt. "That I can't deny," I said. Icy, but not contemptuous enough.

"And it paved the way for these, er . . ."

"UNDEAD."

"In other words, your story enabled them to enter our world?"

"So I already said, I believe." That's better, Freddy.

"Well then, you must give your story a happy ending."

"Huh?"

"It's quite simple," said Marmaduke. "You must enable the Undead to depart."

I stared at him.

"My dear sir, is my reasoning really so hard to follow?" Marmaduke regarded me with extreme condescension. "You must finish your story in such a way as to send the Undead back where they belong."

Chapter Sixteen

MARMADUKE'S IDEA was positively brilliant.

And, above all, so obvious. I had provided Grim Harry and his ferrets with a route from their world to ours, so it ought to be possible for me to send them back the same way. Why hadn't that occurred to any of us, not even Mr. John? Some things are so complicated that simple ideas have no place in them. To put it another way, none of us had seen the forest for the trees.

None of us but Marmaduke. *He* had seen the forest. Why? Because (to be blunt) he was too stupid to see the trees.

For all that, as soon as one examined his idea closely, the forest quickly dissolved into individual trees again.

What did it mean: "You must finish your story in such a way as to send the Undead back where they belong"? *What* must I write that would make Grim Harry and his ferrets disappear forever? They were already in the

process of making themselves at home in our world without the aid of my story. I was confronted by a dense mass of trees. In order to hack my way through them, I would need a kind of **Ma⌐ic ax.**

And that I would find, if at all, in "The Lord of the Ferrets." I must take another good look at the story. It still existed, fortunately. Thanks to my foresight (well, thanks more to my hamsterish reluctance to abandon hard-won stores), the laptop still preserved it in the form of *FSC (Freddy's Secret Copy)*.

"Sir William," I said, "we must save the world — or the Templeton family, at least. Back to the castle!"

In the Great Hall, Sebastian and Annabelle were still busy putting up camp beds. Annabelle paused to watch us with

a frown as Sir William, with me on his back, made for the stairway to the tower.

Upstairs in our tower room, Sir William leaped onto the table and I dismounted. Now to open the laptop and . . .

THE LaPTOP WaS GONE.

The table was completely bare.

"Bertha must have been tidying up in here," I hazarded.

Sir William surveyed the room with his keen eyes. "But I can't see anything resembling a laptop."

"Then Mr. John must have it. Would you mind?" Sir William was already on his way. He bounded up the stairs to Mr. John's room and disappeared inside. I heard him mew, followed by Mr. John's voice: "You want me for something?" Another mew, and they both came down the stairs.

"It's not in Mr. John's room either," Sir William reported. "I suppose I'd better go look for it." And he disappeared through the door.

Mr. John saw at once that the laptop was missing. He scanned the room. "You've no idea where it could be?" he asked. I shook my head. "Strange," he muttered. "Who could . . . Yes, come in!" Someone had knocked.

The door opened and in came Annabelle.

She was holding the laptop out in front of her with both hands.

Mr. John looked at her inquiringly.

"I thought I'd . . ." she began, then suddenly shook her head. "No, that's nonsense. I hid it."

"I see," said Mr. John. "You mean you hid it so Freddy couldn't rewrite his story?"

"No, so he couldn't go on with it. I reckon he's saved a secret copy somewhere in the laptop." She turned to me. "I'm sorry, Freddy, but you must have."

Because I'm an irresponsible, untrustworthy hamster? *I'm* sorry, Annabelle, but I resent that — in spite of your (admittedly divine) scent of chamomile blossom.

She looked at me earnestly. "Yesterday, Freddy, I

came and asked you if you'd written any more of your story."

Right, and I was honest enough to admit that I had.

"Then *you* asked if Grim Harry had appeared to anyone, and I said no."

RIGHT AGAIN. The ferrets hadn't put in another appearance, that's why I still —

"That wasn't true. Someone *did* see Grim Harry that night." Annabelle paused. Then she said, "I did."

Annabelle wasn't just a girl who'd read all the Freddy books with care and smelled divinely of chamomile blossom. She was also a girl who'd seen a member of the Undead and kept her nerve.

"Yes," she said. "Somehow I realized at once that Grim Harry hadn't come to harm me, just to tell me something."

"He speaks a very old-fashioned kind of English, according to your father," Mr. John pointed out. "Could you understand what he said?"

Annabelle shook her head. "Not a hope, though he did sound a bit like some of the old countryfolk around here. But anyway, he didn't say what he wanted, he showed me."

"He showed you?" said Mr. John. "He can show us pictures?"

"Yes. First I saw Freddy here in this room, typing away on the laptop. He looked absolutely real and alive. Then Daddy and Sebastian appeared, also looking real — and alive, but only to begin with. Then Daddy and Sebastian went all pale and motionless, as though they were dead . . ." Annabelle fell silent. Suddenly, I caught the faint but unmistakable scent of fear. Her eyelashes fluttered, and the look in her eyes seemed to reflect what she had felt at the time. She hadn't lost her nerve, but she'd come very close to it.

"You remained calm," said Mr. John. "I guess that's why he didn't harm you. You did the right thing."

Annabelle drew a deep breath, and the scent of fear evaporated. "Anyway, I realized what all this meant: If

Freddy didn't stop writing, Grim Harry would kill Daddy and Sebastian."

JUST a MINUTE.

I pointed to the laptop and Mr. John folded back the screen. *How would he do that?* I typed. *He could appear only when I was writing my story.*

"Who says?" Annabelle looked at me. "What if I'd asked a certain little rodent to stop writing? Could we have relied on him to do so?"

There it was again: the irresponsible, untrustworthy hamster business! Why did she have to keep harping on it?! My fur bristled, slightly but perceptibly. I'd just started to groom myself, feeling thoroughly disgruntled, when I was enveloped in a fragrant cloud of chamomile-blossom scent. My fur flattened itself in an instant.

"And another thing," Annabelle went on. "Grim Harry made it clear that he would also kill Daddy and Sebastian if I told anyone about his latest appearance."

Which put you in a tight spot, I typed.

"**EXACTLY.** I couldn't say anything to you, but I had to get you to stop writing."

So you had no choice.

Annabelle nodded. "I had to erase your story." She shrugged. "But it was no use. A certain rodent was even smarter than I thought." She smiled.

Naturally I made a secret copy, I typed. *Hamsters are not only smart but farsighted.*

She laughed. "Especially when their name is Freddy, eh?" Another cloud enveloped me. I sat up on my haunches and inhaled her fragrance with quivering whiskers.

Mr. John looked at us both in turn. "Well," he said, "see you later." He walked to the door. "I'm going to have a word with your father, Annabelle. We must work out what to do if the Undead attack us."

I quickly pointed in his direction and Annabelle caught on. "Mr. John," she called, "Freddy wants to say something else."

I know *how to get rid of the Undead,* I typed.

Mr. John stared at the screen. "Really?" He pulled up a chair and sat down. "Okay, kid, let's have it."

I proceeded to outline Marmaduke's suggestion. (I made no mention of Marmaduke himself. It would have been too complicated to explain first about the rabbits, then about Marmaduke, and finally about the fact that his brilliant idea had occurred to him only because he'd seen the forest but not the trees.) In conclusion I typed, *But I still don't know* what *I must write in order to send Grim Harry and his ferrets back to their own world forever.*

"Hmm." Mr. John thought a while, then slowly shook his head. "It won't work," he said.

HUH?

"It won't work, kid. Look, the Undead don't *need* your story anymore — they can appear here without it. Why should they let it send them away?"

Fundamentally, he was only confirming my own misgivings. But no hamster readily parts with what he has once garnered — a brilliant idea, for instance. *Mr. John,* I typed, doing my best to convey unshakable confidence, *my instinct tells me that someplace — whether in my story or elsewhere — there's a hidden key, a kind of magic spell. I'm going to find it, and then I'll send the Undead packing.*

"Well, well." Mr. John looked at me. Then he slowly shook his head again. "No!" he said.

What do you mean?

"I mean you won't do anything of the kind," he said firmly. "We can't tell what would happen if you went on with your story. It could be something really terrible." He stared into space for a moment. "No, it's too risky. That's why you won't try to send the Undead away, not on any account, you hear? That's an order. Do we understand each other?"

I nodded.

"Should I lock up the laptop to be on the safe side?"

BELIEVABLE!

This irresponsible, untrustworthy hamster business seemed to be catching on. *No,* I typed curtly.

"Annabelle," said Mr. John, "can I count on you not to try anything?"

She nodded. "I promise."

"Okay." Mr. John got up and went to the door, then paused. "So he really can conjure up pictures," he said, more to himself than us. "Pictures from the present, at least. If he can also show us scenes from the past — well, as Bertha said, 'goodness help us.' " With a final, vigorous nod, he left the room.

Right, now to open the *Freddy's Secret Copy* file. I naturally intended to observe Mr. John's ban, but I was eager to see if my story really did contain something like a magic spell.

All at once, there it was again: the scent of fear. I looked at Annabelle.

She was staring, wide-eyed, into space.

Chapter Seventeen

ANNABELLE CONTINUED TO STAND THERE, staring. After a while she said slowly, "He *can*, you know. Grim Harry *can* show us scenes from the past. I saw one." Abruptly, she shook her head and the scent of fear subsided. "At least, I think I did."

You don't know for sure?

"It was hazy, and it only appeared for a moment." She looked at the door by which Mr. John had left two minutes earlier. "I thought I'd imagined the whole thing, but I've just realized it could have some connection with Grim Harry himself."

What did you see?

"I couldn't make out much, but there were a lot of people, men and women, and all wearing old-fashioned clothes like Grim Harry. They were crowding around a big wooden tub. I couldn't see what was in it, but some of the men were prodding it with sticks. That scared me,

I don't know why." Annabelle stared into space a while longer. Then she said, "That's it. That's all I saw."

What do you think the scene represented? I typed.

She shrugged. "Not a clue. Maybe it was a festival of some kind. Any ideas?"

Sorry. I didn't have a clue either. In retrospect, that surprises me a little. But, as Great-Grandmother used to say, it's easy to be wise after the event.

I'm now going to . . . I stopped short. It would probably be better to wait until Annabelle had left the room. On the other hand,

I wasn't planning to do anything taboo. *I'm now going to retrieve my story,* I went on and explained why.

"What if you really do find the magic spell?" she asked tensely. "I mean, what do we do then?"

Well, well, so she obviously could conceive of ignoring Mr. John's ban. And I? Hmm. *We'll talk about that when the time comes,* I wrote.

I brought up *Freddy's Secret Copy* on the screen and promptly saved it afresh as *The Lord of the Ferrets.*

Just then I heard someone open the door behind me. Mr. John?! I was about to exit the file in double-quick time when I thought, No! All I'd meant to do was look at it. I turned around.

Sebastian was standing in the doorway.

"So here you are," he said to Annabelle. "Shirking camp-bed duties, eh?"

"**NONSENSE!**" Annabelle snapped. "Anyway, we're almost through."

"Calm down, only kidding." Sebastian came over to the table. "Hey, Freddy," he said, pointing to the screen,

"is that your story?" He grinned.
"Sending Grim Harry away, are
you?" He wagged his finger at me.
"That's against orders!"

I stared at him.

He laughed. "Only kidding," he
repeated. "I heard Mr. John telling Daddy."
He turned serious. "Don't worry, I won't blab."

"I should hope not," said Annabelle. "Besides,
you're wrong. Freddy doesn't intend to do
anything he's been forbidden to do. He's
looking for something, that's all." And she
told him about my theory that the story contained a kind
of magic spell capable of sending the Undead back into
their own world.

217

"I see." Sebastian ran his eyes over the words on the screen. "You made most of this up yourself, didn't you?"

I opened a second window on the screen and wrote, *Yes, that's what authors do.*

"Well," he said, "if I were looking for something that would really work, it wouldn't be in any made-up story. It would be in something that really happened."

It was clear that Sebastian hadn't remained a fan of exciting stories for long. Nonfiction had reclaimed his affections.

So where, pray, should I look? I retorted. *Any ideas?*

"Yes," he said.

WHaT?

"I *do* have an idea."

Really? I typed. *I can hardly wait to hear it.*

"I'm surprised you didn't think of it yourself."
Sebastian paused. He was clearly
trying to heighten the

suspense. "It's obvious you'll need to go looking in one particular book. Any idea which?"

I was wrong. Sebastian was still a fan of exciting stories. *Well, which???* I typed.

Then he said, "The one my father mentioned: *The Chronicle of the Barony of Templeton* — the one in the castle library."

"Castle library" sounded like a big room lined with towering bookshelves bearing masses of volumes arranged side by side, each neatly labeled on the spine with letters and numerals.

Templeton Castle's

library was a poky little room containing a worn old sofa, a rickety table, and two bookshelves. The books on them were old and dusty, and none bore a label.

Annabelle sighed. "Oh dear, they aren't classified."

"CLASSIFIED?" said Sebastian.

"You know, with a number on the back corresponding to a card in a card index, so you can find them quickly. We'll have to take them out one by one and read the titles." She sighed again. "There must be at least two hundred of them."

The library lay at the far end of a passage leading to the tower stairway, so we'd been able to reach it without having to pass through the Great Hall, where we might have been stopped by one of the grown-ups.

On the way there we encountered Sir William, who was delighted to hear that the laptop had turned up again. Now he could abandon his fruitless search and stand guard over the rabbit warren. "You never know, old boy," he told me with a rather rueful smile, "maybe those ferrets *will* find me something of a deterrent."

It was getting dark by now. The library's ceiling light didn't work, but luckily there was a rather dim table lamp. Sebastian turned it on.

"Hey," he exclaimed, "that must be it!" He went over to one of the shelves and pulled out a thick, leather-bound volume, which he opened at the title page. Sure enough, the title read: *Curious and Remarkable Sentences of Death in Ancient Times*.

Meantime, Annabelle had put me on the table and opened the laptop. I started it up and typed, *Yes, this is the collection from which I got the case of Grim Harry.*

"Cool," said Sebastian. He started turning the pages. "Whereabouts is it?"

"We need to find *The Chronicle of the Barony* too,"

Annabelle told us. "I'll look on this shelf and you two try the other."

Sebastian removed the books from our shelf, one by one, and opened them so I could read the titles.

The first was a thick, leather-bound old tome dated 1778: *Sermons of Moderate Length, One for Each Sunday of the Year, Composed for the Use of Priests, Especially in Country Parishes, by the Reverend Philip Wraysbury, Chaplain to the Baron of Templeton.* I shook my head, and Sebastian replaced the volume.

The next book was another old tome, but it wasn't leather-bound and looked pretty battered, as if someone had used it for an inappropriate purpose — to prop up a table with a worm-eaten leg, for instance. The date was 1783 and the title read: *Notable Occurrences in the Barony of Templeton, Collected and Arranged in Chronological Order, for the Edification and Instruction of the Reader, by the Reverend Philip Wraysbury.* Hmm, that sounded quite interesting, but could it be the chronicle itself? Just a minute. Wraysbury? That's right, the parson. Hey! Wasn't a parson supposed to have written the chronicle? I turned over a few pages. I'd assumed that a chronicle was a kind of history book, but this looked more like a collection of anecdotes. I didn't want to make a fool of myself in front of Sebastian by sounding a false alarm. The word *chronological* made me wonder, though. I darted over to the laptop. *We may have something here,* I typed, and wrote the title on the screen.

"**THaT MUST BE iT!**"Annabelle exclaimed. "We've found the chronicle!"

"It says 'chronological,' not 'chronicle,'" Sebastian objected.

"Yes, but it's the same thing. A chronicle records things chronologically, which means in the order they occurred. Don't stare at me like that!" Annabelle glared at us. "I looked it up in the dictionary once, okay?"

Okay, Annabelle. The smarter the girl, the more estimable the hamster privileged to revel in her scent of chamomile blossom.

Annabelle had started leafing through the chronicle. "It happened in 1593, didn't it?" I nodded, and she went on turning the pages. "Ah, here we are: Anno Domini 1545, then 1567, and then" — she turned over another page — "Anno Domini 1601 . . . Just a minute." She turned back again. "Bother! There's a page missing."

It took me a moment to grasp the truth.

I dashed over to the book. On the left was the heading: *Anno Domini 1567.* So the text on the right-hand page was the continuation of the missing one. I ran my eye over it, and there it was: the story of Grim Harry. I ran back to the laptop and typed, *Grim Harry! Top of the right-hand page!*

"Great," Annabelle said and started reading. I ran back to the book and read along with her.

"Hey," said Sebastian, "that's not fair! Let me see. I want to know what it says too."

So Annabelle read the text aloud (with me always a little ahead of her):

Albeit they were only Beasts devoid of Understanding, the Common Folk treated them in a most un-Christian Fashion. This Occurrence, like the whole of those Proceedings, has been much talked of since, and has lingered in the Memory of the Local Inhabitants to the Present Day.

But now it was Time for the Wicked Poacher to undergo his Harsh but Just and Well-Merited Punishment. At the Behest of His Lordship the Baron, Grim Harry, his Arms having been bound, was consigned to the Hangman, who stationed him beneath the Gibbet.

So far from shewing Remorse, however, the Poor Sinner swore aloud that he would never rest throughout Eternity until he had revenged himself on his Judge and his Judge's Descendants.

Notwithstanding this Impenitent and vengeful Oath, he ascended the Ladder and donned the Noose without Demur. After which the Hangman thrust him off, thereby condemning him to Death by the Rope.

Just then, a Terrible Storm broke. The Sky was instantly rent by Shafts of Lightning so numerous and Peals of Thunder so deafening that the Common Folk took Fright and began to flee. But His Lordship the Baron rose and, in a Loud Voice, commanded them to turn back and watch Grim Harry meet his Death on the Gibbet as an Example to All. At that very Moment . . .

NO, STOP! I raced to the laptop as fast as I could. *Stop!* I typed. *Don't read on!*

Annabelle stopped short. "What's wrong?"

For heaven's sake don't read the rest aloud! I wrote. *Grim Harry might appear!*

The other two stared first at the screen and then at me.

It's too soon, I went on. *First I must work out how to do it.*

"Freddy," Annabelle said slowly, "what are you talking about, exactly?"

I'm talking about what the book says next, I typed. *About how I can send Grim Harry away. I'm talking about the magic spell.*

CHAPTER EIGHTEEN

ANNABELLE AND SEBASTIAN stared at the screen.

After a while Annabelle said, "Freddy, do you realize what you've just written?"

Of course, I typed. *What about it?*

"You've said you're going to try to send Grim Harry away."

True. There it was in black and white. I'd made the decision without thinking.

No, wrong. There'd been nothing to decide, because there was no alternative.

"What about Mr. John's ban?"

See how the story ends, I wrote. *Then answer that question yourself.*

She proceeded to read the rest of the text. When she'd finished it she would have a choice between precisely three answers: Either we obeyed the ban, or we consulted Mr. John, or —

"We'll do it, and without asking Mr. John first."

Well! Annabelle wasn't just a girl who'd read all the Freddy books with care and smelled divinely of chamomile blossom, she was also . . . But I think I already wrote something like that. I applauded her decision with a nod, but I couldn't help asking, *What makes you say that?*

"Because what's written there isn't just a magic spell, it's a kind of chute. If we can lure Grim Harry onto it, he'll slide back into his own world whether he wants to or not. We've simply got to try. Why ask Mr. John first? If he says yes, it'll amount to what we're doing anyway. If he says no, we'll have to do it just the same, so better not ask him."

229

"What's this chute you're talking about?" asked Sebastian. **"MiND TELLiNG ME?"**

Annabelle shook her head. "We mustn't say it out loud. Freddy's right: It could make Grim Harry appear too soon."

And that, I amplified, *is why I mustn't write it on the screen either. Sorry, Sebastian.*

He frowned. "All right, Freddy," he said at length. "I've no idea how you plan to send Grim Harry away, but I know one thing: If it doesn't work, we're in big trouble. If not all of us, certainly me and Daddy, so I'd sooner we had a talk about it first, okay?"

That was just what I'd wanted to avoid. I was the one who had discovered the magic spell, after all. More important, I was the only one who could use it. And now, all kinds of people were butting in and trying to tell me how to proceed.

All right, so "all kinds of people" were only Annabelle and Sebastian. Annabelle was something else. Anyone she teamed up with could think himself lucky, especially when he was a hamster with a sensitive nose. And Sebastian? If I were scared, like him, that a member of the Undead might rip off my head or do something equally unpleasant to me, I would naturally want to be brought into the picture.

It was precisely then that I felt a sense of responsibility. I'd scarcely been aware of it till now, I admit (maybe I really was an irresponsible creature), but it suddenly descended on me like a lead weight — on me, Freddy, the little golden hamster. Although I didn't want to shirk that responsibility, I realized that one false move on my part, however small, would seal the fate of a lot of humans and animals (myself included, incidentally).

SIR WILLIAM R.I.P.

FREDDY R.I.P.

MR. JOHN

ANNABELLE

ENRICO

Look, I typed, *maybe we should let Mr. John in on this after all. Earlier adventures of mine have taught me that it might be a good thing to . . . No?*

Annabelle had firmly shaken her head. "Freddy, you know Grim Harry far better than anyone else. What advice could Mr. John give you? He could only say 'Do it' or 'Don't do it.' " She looked at me. "Or are you trying to put the responsibility onto him? That wouldn't be fair."

It was true — true because I knew myself far better in this respect than Mr. John.

VERY WELL. Freddy the golden hamster hereby accepted responsibility for the fate of all the occupants of Templeton Castle, human and animal.

But my heart began to pound even so. It started racing — a most unhealthy condition for a hamster, because our hearts operate at high revs at the best of times. The stress wasn't exactly life-threatening, but still.

Just then, Sebastian said, "Freddy, you're assuming

that Grim Harry will appear if you summon him with your story, but he doesn't *have* to, does he? What if he won't come at all?"

E WAS RiＧHT! My heart almost stopped now. Why hadn't I thought of that? If a person didn't come, you could hardly send him away. To reassure Sebastian (and myself) I typed, *He's bound to come. Out of curiosity, let's say.*

Sebastian nodded. "And the ferrets? How will you send *them* away?"

Okay, he had a right to know, but all these incessant questions were beginning to get on my nerves. I was about to fob off Sebastian with "They'll disappear with their master" when something flashed through my mind. *There's a special solution for the ferrets,* I replied. *I'm sure I've already spotted it, but I can't recall what it is for the moment. Don't worry,* I added, *I will when the time comes.*

Sebastian stared at his sister in silence. "Look," she told him, "you could ask another hundred questions and you'd get a hundred answers, but they'd all be based on guesswork. These things can't be worked out like two plus two equals four." She paused. Then she said, "Personally, I'm sure Freddy will manage it."

Thanks, Annabelle, I needed that.

"So am I," said Sebastian, but I can't pretend his eyes shone with conviction.

"But there's one point we must clear up at all costs," said Annabelle. "How will Grim Harry know what you tell him — what you write on the screen, I mean?"

I was about to reply "He'll read it . . ." But that was nonsense, of course. In Grim Harry's day no peasant ever learned to read. *He always turns up when I'm writing. He senses it somehow.*

"He may know *when* you're writing," said Annabelle, "but does he also know *what* you're writing?"

That really did seem unlikely. What next? **I HaDN'T THE FaiNTEST iDEa.** *What do we do now?* I typed.

"It's quite simple, Freddy. Think."

One moment . . . I stared at her. Surely she couldn't mean . . .

Annabelle nodded. "You write your story, and I'll read it aloud to him."

You'd really do that? But it could be dangerous for you!

"For you too. Well, is it a deal?"

What a question! I typed, *You bet!* and Annabelle couldn't help laughing.

"What about me?" Sebastian asked. "What can *I* do?"

"You can't do anything here in the library," Annabelle told him. "In fact, you mustn't stay here. You must go to the Great Hall."

"You think I'm scared."

"No, I don't, but what if something happens to me and Freddy? There's got to be someone who's in the know. And if the grown-ups take it into their heads to look for us, you must put them off somehow. Okay?"

"Okay." Sebastian seemed distinctly relieved. "To be honest, I wasn't too keen on seeing Grim Harry again in any case." He glanced around. "Are you planning to do it in here?"

Annabelle looked at me inquiringly and I nodded. The library was so remote from the rest of the castle, we wouldn't be interrupted. It mightn't be a spacious ballroom, but it was quite big enough for me to lead Grim Harry in a dance (my little joke).

"If it won't annoy you too much, Freddy," said Sebastian, "I have one more question to ask before I go."

Which is?

"What about the laptop's battery? It'd be pretty silly if the juice ran out just as you were sending Grim Harry to kingdom come."

The battery was still half charged. That would almost certainly be good enough, but I temporarily turned off the laptop to be on the safe side — though not, of course, before Annabelle and I had discussed everything and made the necessary arrangements.

It was dark by now. The table lamp dimly illuminated

the part of the room where the table, sofa, and bookshelves were, but the area near the door was bathed in gloom. Was that where Grim Harry would appear?

I had asked Annabelle to turn the laptop around so that I didn't have to write with my back to the pool of darkness. Annabelle herself had sat down on the sofa. This would enable her to read what was written on the screen with ease, aside from having the table in front of her as a barrier. "I feel a bit safer here," she said, "though I know it's no real defense against Grim Harry."

I, on the other hand, was reasonably well protected from the ferrets. They'd been worrying me. What if they turned up before Grim Harry did and promptly sprang at me? Annabelle would try to shoo them away. "I don't see any problem there," she said blithely. She'd never set eyes on the monstrous creatures, of course, but I didn't point this out for fear of alarming her unnecessarily.

That was why I didn't confide another worry of mine: Would my command center SOUND THE aLaRM, and, if it did, what effect on me would it have? There were two possibilities: I would either rear up and bare my teeth — I could handle that — or lie flat on my back and play possum. That would put an end to "Operation Banish Grim Harry" — and perhaps to us.

But my biggest worry of all was something that obviously hadn't occurred to Annabelle, or she would have said something: Could the Undead watch what was going on in the world of the living? Were they capable of switching to "Receive" at any moment, so to speak, and listening in on us?

If so, we might as well give up. Any attempt to lure Grim Harry onto our "chute" and send him back where he belonged would then be as pointless as trying to nail Jell-O to a wall.

In fact, when I came to think of it . . .

I had to stop before sheer worry turned my paws to jelly and I couldn't write a word.

I nodded to Annabelle. She nodded back.

I turned on the laptop.

And retrieved *The Lord of the Ferrets*.

Good. Where had I gotten to?

They were waiting for him.

Grim Harry's cottage was full of the Baron's armed retainers.

He hadn't the slightest chance of escaping. . . .

How should the story continue? I'd wondered at this point. Should I now describe Grim Harry's capture, or would it be better to skip that and go straight on to describe how the Baron sentences him to death?

Judgment day had come.

The Baron had summoned all the peasants and townsfolk in the county to assemble on Gallows Hill. For this one day, he had exempted them from the forced labor that all his subjects had to perform. He had also seen to it that they were plied with food and drink. Moreover, there were many sights for them to see. The Baron had spread word of the forthcoming execution, not only in his own domain but in those adjoining it, so that numerous strangers had flocked to the scene, together with traveling folk such as peddlers, jugglers, and acrobats. In consequence, the atmosphere that reigned on Gallows Hill resembled that of a fairground.

But the brow of the hill was ringed by a detachment of armed guards — not that anyone cared to approach it, for the common folk believed that misfortune would attend those who ventured too close to the gallows erected on the summit.

People also preserved their distance from the platform erected nearby, for that was where the Baron, together with his family and retainers, had taken their places. Soon a trumpet call would herald the start of the proceedings.

Before that, however, a roll on the drums
was heard. It came from an open space below
the summit, and the people who thronged there
saw, in the midst of that open space, a big
wooden tub. . . .

A big wooden tub . . . Annabelle had mentioned one.
A big wooden tub had formed part of the scene Grim
Harry had shown her. . . .

"Freddy," she whispered.

When I turned to look, she signaled to me with
a jerk of the head. I darted to the other side
of the table, thrust my head slowly
over the edge, and looked
down. And there on the
floor, within range of
the lamplight, were two
shapes.

The ferocious ferrets
had appeared.

CHaPTER NINETEEN

THE FEROCIOUS FERRETS?

They certainly didn't look ferocious at the moment, and my mental command center had issued no alert. They were sitting quite still with their mouths closed. They weren't snarling, and the jangle of the bells on their collars was very faint. I couldn't detect a hint of blood-lust in their demeanor. Although they must have seen me long before, they weren't looking at me. Their eyes were fixed on the place where the lamplight ended.

They were staring into the pool of darkness.

And, while I was peering down at them and wondering, a picture took shape in the gloom. But it wasn't like a photograph — the people in it were moving around. It resembled a movie, but it wasn't a movie either; it was like real people seen from a distance. I could hear them too. The air was filled with the kind of hum that a big crowd makes.

Then the scene changed.

As if I were the lens of a mobile camera, I glided past people dressed in old-fashioned clothes, heard unintelligible cries and scraps of conversation, and came to a sudden stop.

AND THERE WAS THE BIG WOODEN TUB.

I turned to look at Annabelle. She was gazing spellbound in the direction of the scene. There was no doubt about it: We were both seeing the same thing. She noticed me looking at her and nodded: The tub was the one Grim Harry had shown her.

It was chest-high and so big that Linda's car would have fit into it with ease. Masses of people were standing around it with a look of expectancy that conveyed there would soon be some sight worth seeing. More and more of them crowded around the tub until it was hemmed in by jostling figures.

And then some men with wooden poles appeared.

They must have numbered about half a dozen, all wearing caps and smocks of leather. The spectators made way for them, and they stationed themselves around the tub. The crowd steadily swelled. Even some distance away, people were now standing shoulder to shoulder.

The imaginary camera took us in closer, until we were right beside the tub. In the midst of the spectators and their unintelligible hubbub of voices, we saw that the tub was filled with water. But not completely: The surface was an arm's length below the rim.

All at once our viewpoint changed. Willingly, almost deferentially, the onlookers stood aside to let two men approach the tub: an elderly man in a colorful tunic with a sword at his side, followed by a younger man wearing a leather smock and carrying a sack on his shoulder. The sack was moving — or rather, something *inside* it was moving.

Suddenly, a cry pierced the hum of voices around us. Issuing from two throats simultaneously, **iT WaS a SHRiLL CRY OF TERROR —** but not a human cry, and when I looked down I saw that the ferrets had risen on their haunches, mouths open and fur bristling.

By now the men had reached the tub and mounted

a small platform erected beside it. In response to an order from the older man, the younger proceeded to untie the neck of the sack. The crowd fell silent.

"What is it?" I heard Annabelle whisper. "What's happening?" I turned to look at her. She was gazing at the scene, wide-eyed. "What's happening?" she repeated. "What are they doing?"

The men on the platform picked up the sack between them. Raising it high, they turned it upside down and shook it as hard as they could.

OUT TUMBLED THE FERRETS.

They fell into the tub, and during the instant they were falling we saw that their forelegs were free but their hind legs were bound together.

The crowd uttered a great yell as they hit the water with a splash.

The ferrets surfaced. Frantically paddling with their forepaws, they swam to the edge of the tub, but when they got there and strove to cling to the wooden sides, the men armed with poles thrust them out into the middle once more.

The spectators bellowed.

Desperately, the ferrets made repeated attempts to reach the side of the tub, only to be fended off again and again. It was clear how the whole thing would end.

And all the time the people around the tub continued to bawl and bellow. They cheered on the ferrets, some in delight at this cruel spectacle, but others, as one could tell from the coins that changed hands, because they were laying bets on how long the creatures would survive. None of them seemed to know the meaning of pity.

But suddenly, drowning their cries, someone shouted, "**STOP!**"

It was Annabelle.

STOP IT AT ONCE!" she cried, jumping up off the sofa. She ran around the table and out into the midst of the scene. "Don't any of you feel sorry for them?"

And the scene vanished as she spoke.

It disappeared in a flash, as if someone had thrown a switch, leaving her in darkness. The glow from the table lamp did not reach her.

And then I picked up the scent.

A scent of ferret.

I recognized the smell at once, so pungent that it stung my nostrils.

I peered down. There they were, looking up at me. Their eyes glittered with the light of battle, but they were grinning. Cruncher and Muncher were grinning at me: They knew that I knew what had just happened.

"All right, you two," I told them. "That's it. Now get lost, okay?"

247

The ferrets looked at each other. Their grins widened — and suddenly they vanished.

The ferocious ferrets had returned to their own world.

"To their own world?" Annabelle said when I wrote this on the screen. "But in their own world they were dead." She stared at me. "You mean they're really dead now?"

I guess so, I typed, *but they've been that way for centuries.*

Annabelle debated this for a moment. "Yes, but they may have returned to the world of the Undead."

I doubt it. You released them, so to speak.

"I WHAT?"

Now it was my turn to stare. She didn't know what she'd done!

You released the ferrets, I typed, *because you came out with the right magic spell.* After a moment I added, *But please don't ask me what it was.*

So all that remained was to send Grim Harry away too.

We had resumed our places, Annabelle on the sofa behind the table and I behind the laptop.

I was in good spirits. Getting rid of Grim Harry ought to be as easy as banishing the ferrets had been, especially since we already had a magic spell for him. Now that he had shown us the tub scene, there was no doubt that he would appear.

Or had he already done so?

I peered around the laptop and into the darkness. No, not as far as I could see, but anyway, Annabelle would tell me when he did. I opened a second window on the screen and arranged the two windows so that the one on the left displayed my story and the new, blank one was on the right. In this I wrote, *Annabelle, I'll go on with my story in the left-hand window and type what I want to tell you here, on the right.*

She nodded. "And I'll take care not to read it out loud. That way, we'll trick Grim Harry."

Fine, I typed. *Now I'll go on with the story, okay?*

But she didn't reply. She was staring past me, WIDE-EYED.

And there, roughly at the spot where the ferrets had disappeared, stood Grim Harry.

I was seeing him for the very first time.

He was even taller than I'd thought, but his clothes looked just as I'd imagined. I had also formed a precise mental picture of his piercing gaze and grim expression, though not of his ghastly, gray-green pallor.

I had heard the descriptions given by Sebastian and his father, Annabelle, and Bertha, and Grim Harry had been so often talked of in recent days that he seemed quite familiar to me. Above all, I had been expecting him.

I could imagine, however, that if he had suddenly appeared out of the blue, without my expecting him, the effect on me would have been hair-raising in the literal sense.

I turned to look at Annabelle. She was still staring at him, but she seemed quite calm.

Suddenly, from behind me, came:

"BARON'S DAUGHTER, YOU SENT MY FERRETS AWAY!"

CHaPTER TWENTY

I SPUN AROUND.

Grim Harry was standing there as before, a tall, sinister figure, but his face looked even grimmer than before, and there was a menacing note in his loud, gruff voice.

"Have you learned to speak like us?" Annabelle asked, sounding merely surprised. His note of menace had clearly escaped her.

"As you can hear," said Grim Harry. His voice hardened. "You have banished my ferrets, not only from your own world but from the world of the Undead as well. I did not want that, Baron's daughter!"

He had grown angry. Annabelle stared at him in alarm, then at me. Freddy, the expert on the Undead, was in demand! I had to calm him down — somehow. *Annabelle,* I wrote in the right-hand window, *ask him what he did want.*

She did so.

"I wanted to show how badly the Baron had treated me, in the first place by drowning my ferrets. But then you interfered!" He was becoming steadily more irate. My question had been a mistake. I needed a more innocuous topic of conversation.

Hurriedly (for want of a better idea), I typed, *Tell him: Freddy the hamster says you look just as he imagined you.* Surprisingly enough, **THIS WORKED.** Grim Harry nodded slowly. "Except that Freddy the hamster does not resemble a hamster. I know all the beasts of the field and forest, but never have I seen a hamster with fur of that color, still less one so small."

Hmm. I had to let that pass, unfortunately. Under present circumstances, I felt it was pointless to try to explain to this sixteenth-century poacher that only big, uncouth field hamsters were known in the Europe of his day, and that dainty little *golden* hamsters had yet to reach there from Syria.

Besides, he was growing angry again. "Show yourself, hamster!" he said brusquely. "Come out from behind that light-book!" I did so. "Of course I look the way you imagined! Where do you think they came from, your ideas about me and my world? Eh?"

JUST a MiNUTE . . . Did what I had written . . . ?

Grim Harry nodded. "They all came from me. Do you remember how your paws twitched? I was guiding them while you wrote." His twisted grin looked ghastly on that gray-green face. "Not really, of course. I cannot read and write, but the pictures you saw as you wrote were put into your head by me."

For an author who prided himself on his powers of imagination, that was a bitter pill to swallow. So all my lovely mental images had been supplied by a member of the Undead! Even so, I was the one who had put them into words. That made me half an author, if not more.

But wait! There was something wrong here! How could he . . .

"How could you put pictures into Freddy's head?"

Annabelle demanded. "They couldn't appear until he started writing."

"Clever girl." Grim Harry gave another gruesome grin. "The world of the Undead is not entirely cut off from the world of the living. I was able to achieve a little, even from there — I appeared here as soon as the hamster started to write. From then on, he danced to my tune. But that's enough talk!" he bellowed abruptly. "I no longer need any hamster in order to reach your world — nor in order to do what I must!" He was furious once more.

His erratic moods were beginning to alarm me. I still felt confident of my ability to banish him forever by pronouncing my magic spell, but for that I would need the right opportunity. Until now we

had merely reacted to his fluctuating emotions. What if he suddenly lost his temper and crushed me in his fist? I glanced at Annabelle. She seemed calm, but I thought I detected a flicker of apprehension in her eyes.

aRON'S DaUGHTER! HaMSTER! LOOK HERE!"

Grim Harry pointed into the darkness. And all at once, with his arm still extended, he vanished.

Simultaneously, a scene took shape in the gloom. As before, it was as if what we saw and felt were utterly real. The air was oppressively sultry — I could actually feel it — and we were facing the summit of Gallows Hill. Men-at-arms in tall, pointed helmets had cordoned off the place of execution with their pikes held crosswise. Around this barrier and all down the hillside, close-packed spectators were standing shoulder to shoulder.

The huge crowd was so hushed, crows could be heard cawing in the distance.

We were now taken into the heart of the scene. We glided past silent onlookers craning their necks and peering in the direction we were moving. Then we came to a halt in front of the viewing stand.

This was a simple wooden platform on which rough-hewn benches had been placed, but the people who occupied them were elegantly attired, the women dressed in sumptuous gowns, the men in richly embroidered doublets. In the front row, seated in massive armchairs, were the Baron's wife, son, and daughter. The Baron himself was seated on a low dais, his mountainous frame encased — despite the heat and humidity — in a magnificent, thickly padded doublet with puff sleeves. The plainly dressed individual beside him was rolling up a parchment from which he appeared to have been reading.

Just below the Baron stood Grim Harry. Although not bound, he was flanked by two men in leather smocks, and behind him waited the colorfully dressed man with the sword at his side.

"That must be the executioner," I heard Annabelle whisper. "How awful!" I turned to look at her. She was

sitting there with her hands clasped to her mouth, staring at the scene. I hoped she would keep quiet. Any interruption was bound to arouse Grim Harry's fury.

The Baron rose, holding a thin white wand in his hand. He made a loud announcement in the old-fashioned language I couldn't understand, raised the wand above his head, and snapped it in half. A muffled cry went up from the hundreds of onlookers.

The man with the sword laid his hand on Grim Harry's shoulder. Standing tall and erect, Grim Harry looked up and gave the Baron a long, piercing stare. Then, in response to a command from the executioner, the men in leather smocks bound Grim Harry's hands behind his back and, to a roll on the drums, conducted him to the place of execution. From our position beside the stand we watched him, flanked by his guards, cross the summit of the hill to the gallows.

In the meantime a wind had sprung up. Quite suddenly, clouds began to gather — thick, dark storm clouds. The sun vanished and then reappeared, only to be blotted out once more.

The gibbet loomed up, tall and sinister, in the changing light. Propped against it was a stout ladder, and dangling from the crossbeam was the rope.

Grim Harry had now reached the gibbet and was standing just beneath the noose. He climbed the ladder, followed by the man with the sword. Not a sound came from the crowds surrounding the place of execution.

Just then Annabelle whispered, "I don't want to see it." She repeated the words more loudly, "I don't want to see it." Louder still: "I don't want to see it!" She jumped up and dashed toward the scene — and it vanished. Grim Harry's image had been obliterated.

But he himself had reappeared, seething with rage. **'OU DON'T WANT TO SEE IT?"** he roared. "You *must* see it, Baron's daughter!"

He reached her in two swift strides. Producing a cord from the pouch on his belt, he quickly tied her wrists

together. She seemed paralyzed with fright, and when he took out a cloth, rolled it up, and commanded her to open her mouth, she obeyed as if hypnotized. He thrust the cloth into her mouth and tied the ends together behind her head. Then he pushed her down on the sofa and lashed her ankles to one of the sofa legs. "There, Baron's daughter," he growled. "There's an end to your interruptions."

And I, sitting on the table, had to look on helplessly. I went numb at first, in mind as well as body, but when Grim Harry gagged Annabelle with the cloth, it suddenly dawned on me: We were finished! Annabelle wouldn't be able to read out what I wrote, not anymore. I wouldn't have a chance to use my magic spell. **IT WAS OVER!**

I thought feverishly. In physical terms, of course, a little golden hamster was no match for Grim Harry. I couldn't summon help either, nor was any to be expected. We had made a point of telling Sebastian to keep everyone away. My only hope was to try the magic spell all the same. Perhaps it would get through to Grim

Harry by some telepathic means if I wrote it on the screen. I darted over to the keyboard. How best to begin?

And then I was seized. Grim Harry's enormous fist enclosed me so completely, I couldn't move a paw. I tried to bite him, but he gave me a quick squeeze that drove the breath from my lungs. "I could crush you," he said, "but I'll do that later."

I heard him take something from his pouch, was thrust inside something, heard a click, and found myself in a little wire cage — the sort of mousetrap used for catching mice alive. Grim Harry deposited it on the table. "You may have helped me to enter your world," he said angrily, "but don't imagine I'll let you go free on that account."

He turned to Annabelle. "And you, Baron's daughter, are going to pay the price for having crossed me. I meant to spare you, if the truth be told. You brought this on yourself with that stupid outcry of yours. But as for your father and brother, they must die."

So he didn't intend to kill her. That news rekindled a little glimmer of hope in me. *Any* change in our situation, no matter how small, improved our chances. Perhaps we would still contrive to pronounce the magic spell.

Annabelle, bound and gagged, sat there with her eyes flickering. Once again I caught the faint but unmistakable scent of fear, but she was striving to keep her nerve. The noises coming from under her gag sounded like a question.

"You wish to know why I shall kill your father and your brother?"

She nodded.

"I swore an oath beneath the gallows," Grim Harry said slowly. "It went like this: 'I will never rest throughout death and eternity until I have revenged myself on my judge or his descendants for the injustice done me.' I must keep that oath."

Annabelle shrugged her shoulders inquiringly.

"Why must I? Why can I not forgo my revenge?" Grim Harry remained calm — ominously calm. "Because my oath banished me to the world of the Undead, the realm of the despairing souls whose one desire is to be released — to be allowed to die at last. I have been there ever since. That, Baron's daughter, is a very, very long time — well-nigh an eternity." He paused. "And it avails me nothing that I can visit your world. Even here I remain a member of the Undead." Very quietly, he concluded, "So you see, Baron's daughter, there is no other way.

I must kill your father and your brother." He stood looking down at her.

"But enough of talk!" he roared suddenly. "I shall now do what has to be done!" He was so overcome with fury that my little glimmer of hope faded. "You shall both watch the scene to the very end, so that you know why you have to die!"

You shall *both* . . . One moment . . . Those words sounded as if they had been addressed to Lord Templeton and Sebastian. But if so, it was pointless to show us the scene here in the library. Or could Grim Harry appear in several places at once? **THAT WOULD MEAN . . .**

Just then a shaft of light pierced the gloom near the door.

It came from outside.

The door opened.

And in walked Sebastian.

CHAPTER TWENTY-ONE

IT REALLY WAS SEBASTIAN.

There he stood.

My heart gave a jump. The situation *had* changed —
quite considerably too.

Sebastian shut the door and walked over to the glow
from the table lamp.

What accounted for his sudden appearance? Had he
gone mad? He knew he might run into Grim Harry here.

He must have allowed for this, because he didn't look
particularly scared by the sight of him. But then he saw
Annabelle and uttered a cry of horror.

"Yes, look at your foolish sister. That's what happens
to those who try to thwart me." Grim Harry was clearly
unfazed by Sebastian's arrival on scene. He indicated the
sofa. "SIT DOWN!"

Sebastian, who didn't seem to have noticed that Grim
Harry was speaking modern English, obeyed. He was

still gazing in horror at Annabelle sitting bound and gagged on the sofa beside him.

Although Annabelle couldn't have been feeling too good, she now did something truly magnificent: She looked at Sebastian and shrugged her shoulders — only a little gesture, but it meant: "This is how it is, but don't worry, we'll manage."

And Sebastian nodded. He drew a deep breath and sat up straight.

As if by chance, he glanced at the mousetrap on the table.

Unless I was much mistaken, he gave me an almost imperceptible wink. I began to wonder what it all signified. Had he simply blundered in here, or was it part of some plan?

Annabelle's gesture must have restored Sebastian's confidence, because he looked Grim Harry in the eye with an almost inquisitive air.

Grim Harry's latest fit of temper had yet to subside. "What do you mean by coming in here?" he snapped. "Still, why not? It makes no difference *where* you see the picture." He nodded grimly. "And take it from me: This time you'll watch it to the very end."

"The end?" said Sebastian, gazing at him with big, wondering eyes. "What end?" He seemed genuinely eager to know.

"The end of the picture, of course!"

"But what's that? I mean, *how* does it end?"

"How do you think?" The veins in Grim Harry's neck began to bulge again. "Use your imagination, boy!"

Sebastian continued to gaze at him with eyes like saucers.

"WITH THE HANGING, OF COURSE!"

cried Grim Harry. "With the executioner thrusting me from the ladder! With a fiery flash as if a musket had gone off inside my head! Do you understand?"

Sebastian nodded, rather apprehensively now.

"My last sight in this world," Grim Harry went on,

staring into space, "was of the Baron seated on the platform, his great paunch, his fleshy face, his murderous grin." He shook his head. "That, alas, was all I saw."

Then Sebastian said, "Would you like to see more? Would you like to see what happened next?"

Grim Harry stared at him. "What happened after the hanging, you mean?"

Sebastian nodded.

"What happened on Gallows Hill?"

Sebastian nodded again.

Grim Harry continued to stare at him. "But only the Undead can show pictures from times gone by."

Sebastian shook his head. "So can many of the living. When they know the story of what happened, they can describe it in writing. That's as good as showing pictures — better, even."

"The hamster has already told my story."

"Yes, but there's an old book that tells what happened after the hanging. Freddy could describe that too."

Grim Harry seemed to deliberate. "Old books are no

use to me. I need pictures." His tone was ominously calm. "But don't imagine you can soften my heart, Baron's son. You are doomed to die come what may, you and your father." He looked at Annabelle. "She understands why I have no choice but to kill you. Isn't that so, Baron's daughter?"

Annabelle nodded, but then she gave Sebastian a little, sidelong jerk of the head. "Carry on," it signified.

Sebastian did so. His behavior was very calm, I must admit. Although he may not have grasped quite how seriously Grim Harry meant his threat, that was more than any of us could imagine (with the possible exception of Annabelle). In any case, he said, "It wouldn't hurt you to let Freddy out, would it?"

Grim Harry slowly shook his head. "No," he said, then suddenly snapped again. "But God help him if I see no pictures! I'll crush him to death!" On that note he opened the door of the mousetrap (which — purely for the record — was extremely cramped and disgustingly dirty) and said, "**PROCEED!**"

I darted over to the laptop, which was still displaying my story on the left of the screen and what I'd told Annabelle on the right. *Sebastian,* I wrote, *tell him I need a little time to prepare.*

Sebastian did so, and Grim Harry nodded.

GH really can't read, I typed, then: *Why are you here??? Type your answer. If GH asks, say I can't quite remember what the old book says, but you can, so you'll have to write down the most important details. OK?*

Sebastian nodded. *The pictures appeared in the Great Hall as well,* he typed.

"**HANDS OFF, BARON'S SON!**" Grim Harry bellowed, but he calmed down when Sebastian told him what I'd suggested. "Very well," he growled, eyeing the boy suspiciously. "But I warn you, Baron's son: No tricks! And make haste, the two of you — my patience isn't inexhaustible." He stood there calmly with his arms folded, but he might fly off the handle again at any moment.

WE WOULD HaVE TO HURRY.

Go on! I typed.

I told the grown-ups what you were doing in here, Sebastian wrote. He looked guilty, but I quickly typed, *OK,* and he went on: *Mr. J thought the two pictures ended too soon, so something must be wrong and he was going to go and see.*

"I'm waiting," Grim Harry said darkly.

"I won't be much longer," Sebastian told him. *But I was sure that GH would have attacked the grown-ups,* he wrote, *so I convinced them that you needed my help to write your magic spell, and that I was then the best person to help you.*

Which you certainly have, I typed. (One should always find time to administer a well-deserved pat on the back. And who could tell? It might be the last one Sebastian ever received.) *The only trouble is,* I went on, *I doubt if the spell will work. GH wants pictures. If he doesn't see them, the spell won't work. And what then???*

Sebastian shrugged. *Mr. J, Daddy, and Bertha are waiting outside in the passage,* he wrote, *but what can they do?*

"This is taking too long!" Grim Harry had unfolded his arms.

Sebastian typed, *You* must *send him back! You MUST!*

"**THAT'S ENOUGH!**" cried Grim Harry.

My paws moved like lightning. I had just managed to type *Annabelle must read it aloud!* when Grim Harry grabbed Sebastian and thrust him aside.

"You're deceiving me!" he shouted. "Tell me, this minute, the last thing that animal wrote in the light-book!"

"Why not?" Sebastian said coolly. He even managed a shrug. "He wrote: 'Ask our awe-inspiring visitor to remove the cloth from Annabelle's mouth. She must read my story aloud, or there'll be no pictures.'"

"So I'm awe-inspiring, am I?" Grim Harry's gray-green face contorted itself into another of his frightful grins. "Very well, so be it." He went over to Annabelle and removed the gag. "There. Now I want to see something —BUT FaST!"

I gave Annabelle a nod, and she nodded back. *Please read slowly,* I wrote in the right-hand window. *But make it sound natural. I'll try to write as quickly and fluently as I can, okay?*

"Okay," said Annabelle.

I switched to my story in the left-hand window and read the last words I'd written: . . . a big wooden tub . . .

Well, at least we'd gotten *that* part over. All right, here we go.

I collected my thoughts.

First I recalled what I'd read in the chronicle. Then I reviewed Grim Harry's second picture in my mind's eye. I saw the Baron snap the wand in two, saw the

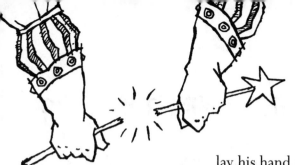

executioner lay his hand on the prisoner's shoulder, saw Grim Harry conducted to the gallows, saw him climb the ladder and stand there with the noose around his neck. I saw him staring across at the Baron, and I remembered the changing light and the gathering storm clouds.

I looked up from the screen. Grim Harry was gazing at us expectantly. He really wanted to know what had happened after his execution. He was waiting for my pictures.

On no account, I realized, must I attempt to describe what he'd actually experienced in his final moments. If what I wrote failed to match his recollections of them, he would never believe the rest of my story.

I would have to begin after his death — immediately after it.

I started to write.

275

Chapter Twenty-Two

The instant the rope went taut, the onlookers uttered a cry that rang out far across the countryside. And, while Grim Harry's body swung to and fro, they eagerly proceeded to discuss what they had seen. The hum of voices swept across Gallows Hill like a storm wind.

The nobles on the viewing stand were also deep in excited conversation. They had all jumped up when the hangman thrust the ladder away from beneath Grim Harry. All, that is to say, except the Baron. He had continued to sit in his chair on the dais, though his hands had tightened on the chair's arms at the moment of execution. Now he was sitting back, a veritable mountain of flesh, surveying the crowd that was milling around below him. Most of those present were subjects of his for whom Grim Harry's execution was intended to serve as an example. "Take careful note," he muttered, and a smile flitted across his fleshy face. "Thus ends any person who dares to oppose the Baron Templeton." He looked across at the gallows . . .

Annabelle's voice died away. I cast a quick glance at Grim Harry. He was standing absolutely still, listening. More than that, he was staring into the far distance. He could picture the scene.

Grim Harry's body continued to swing, but now it was the wind that propelled it to and fro. It was swinging in the wind that had suddenly developed into a gale. The dense, low clouds that had first appeared in ones and twos when Grim Harry was escorted to the gallows were now obscuring the entire sky. It had gone dark — awesomely dark. The storm would soon break. People looked in all directions. Where could they find shelter? There was none to be had on the bare summit of Gallows Hill. Here and there, people began to drift away from the place of execution.

The Baron had risen from his chair. He didn't like what he saw. He had planned this execution with care, intending it to be a spectacle his underlings would not forget in a hurry, and now they showed signs of melting away. He summoned a trumpeter who had been waiting beside the platform.

I took another look at Grim Harry. He was still staring into space, but his fists were clenched.

The Baron pointed to the men-at-arms who were still cordoning off the place of execution with their pikes held crosswise. It was clear that he wished them to prevent the common folk from leaving Gallows Hill. The trumpeter raised his instrument and prepared to give them the signal.

Just then, the first shaft of lightning hit the ground.

It came straight out of the black clouds above Gallows Hill, accompanied by a thunderclap so deafening that it almost rent the eardrums. More shafts of lightning and peals of thunder followed in quick succession. Then the rain came down — a cloudburst of such magnitude that it might have heralded a second Great Flood.

Everyone fled.

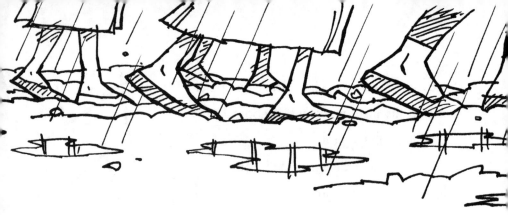

They took to their heels, pushing, shoving, and jostling. "Away! Save yourselves!" they cried. The tumult that arose was reminiscent of a battlefield. The dignitaries on the viewing stand fled too, their fine garments sodden with rain. Like all the rest, they had but a single thought: to leave Gallows Hill as quickly as possible.

The Baron alone stood his ground. He stood there in the pelting rain, arms raised. "Stop!" he cried above the thunder. "Stop! I command you!" he bellowed at the fleeing multitude. "Stay where you are! I, your lord and master, command it!"

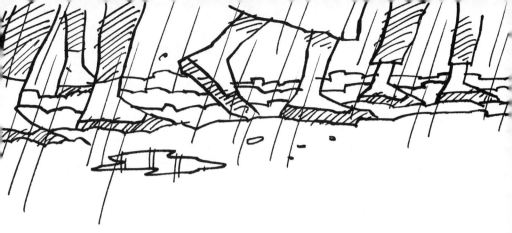

At that moment the thunderstorm ceased.
No more lightning, no more peals of thunder,
just the hiss and roar of the rain.

"I, your lord, command you to return!"

One or two people paused and looked back.

"Come back! Your lord commands it!"

More people came to halt, and a few turned
back.

"I shall visit my wrath on those who go!
Anyone who fails to remain will pay dearly."

Most of the spectators had halted by now,
and many retraced their steps. The downpour
was subsiding, the sky brightening . . .

I heard a deep-chested groan and looked up. Grim Harry's face was contorted. . . .

The Baron pointed to the gallows. Grim Harry's body was gently swinging in what remained of the wind. "Behold!" he cried. "That will show you what becomes of anyone who fails to obey me, your liege lord!"

The Baron continued to stand there with his arms outstretched.

The spectators looked at the Baron, then at the gallows, then back at the Baron.

And then, from out of the inky clouds that continued to loom overhead, a thunderbolt descended.

There were a few who later boasted that they alone saw what happened, but they were notorious windbags who always bragged of being the only ones to witness something.

It was, in fact, seen by almost everyone on Gallows Hill that day.

The shaft of lightning that darted from the clouds, accompanied by an earsplitting clap of thunder, struck the viewing stand fair and square.

More precisely, it struck the dais on which stood the Baron's armchair.

More precisely still, it struck the Baron himself.

All that remained of him was a heap of ashes. Was that . . .

"STOP!"

I broke off. Annabelle's voice died away.

I held my breath.

Grim Harry stood rooted to the spot, still staring into space. At length we heard him whisper, "Was that . . . my revenge? Is that how my judge was punished

for the injustice he did me?" He stared into space for a moment longer, then:

"I'm avenged!" he cried suddenly, throwing up his arms. EAVEN ITSELF HAS AVENGED ME!"

I breathed a sigh of relief. The magic spell had found its mark at last. We'd done it!

Suddenly, I caught a whiff of something.

It was an unfamiliar scent. I had never smelled anything like it before. My nose was invaded by such a terrible stench, I could have cried out in pain.

"What's this?" Grim Harry had lowered his arms. "What's this?" he repeated. "What's happening to me?" He stood there as if listening to something within himself.

The stench intensified. Annabelle and Sebastian, who could now smell it too, started to gasp and retch.

Grim Harry looked over at us. "It will soon pass," he said. "I shall be gone before long." He nodded in confirmation. "I can now return to my own world. I was banished to the world of the Undead because, by

285

swearing that oath beneath the gallows, I sacrificed my soul's salvation in return for revenge. I had to atone for that sin."

He was beginning to dissolve. "Forgive my somewhat sinister conduct — do not think too ill of me. I'll leave you all in peace hereafter."

Almost transparent now, Grim Harry gave one more frightful grin. "No offense, little hamster, but . . ." He raised his arm and pointed in my direction. That was the last I saw of him.

The next thing I saw was a fiery flash.

I didn't hear the bang that accompanied it.

Why not? **BECAUSE I WAS OUT LIKE A LIGHT.**

CHapter TWeNTY-THRee

"FREDDY?"

Who was that? Grim Harry? If so, why had he suddenly taken to calling me Freddy? Why did my head ache so?

"He moved! He's coming around!"

Gee, how my head ached! And what was that smell?

"Freddy, please open your eyes. It's me."

Annabelle! It was Annabelle, but where was her heavenly scent of chamomile blossom? She smelled of charred plastic. And of something else — something quite appalling. . . .

Grim Harry! She smelled of Grim Harry!

I opened my eyes with an effort.

"aT LaST!"

Annabelle was smiling down at me. Where was I? On the library table, and standing around me, in addition to Annabelle, were Sebastian, Lord Templeton, Bertha, and

Mr. John. Except that Mr. John wasn't standing; he was sitting on the sofa.

"Hello, kid," he said with an approving nod. "That was good work. Grim Harry has gone. Everything's fine."

Excellent, but what about my headache? Why was my nose sending out false signals? That stench couldn't possibly be genuine. . . .

"If you're wondering what the smell is," Mr. John went on, "it's the remains of Grim Harry — and the laptop."

What?! I tried to stand up.

"Relax, kid," said Mr. John, and Annabelle started to tickle the back of my neck. That was even better than a chamomile-blossom shower, so I stretched out on my tummy. Who cared about the stench or my headache? I shut my eyes and drifted off into paradise.

Sebastian said, "I think a piece of the laptop must have hit Freddy on the head."

"Crumble half an aspirin into his food," said Lord Templeton, "and he'll be fine by tomorrow."

"Well, if you ask me," Bertha put in, "that cut needs some ointment on it. It must hurt."

YOU BET IT HURT! And that frightful stench . . . I left paradise behind and came down to earth with a bump. I opened my eyes and struggled to my feet.

And there on the table in front of me lay what had once been the laptop. It couldn't be said to have disintegrated, because its components had been fused into a single lump, and the lump was still smoking.

"That was Grim Harry's doing," said Sebastian. "He fried it before he left — with a thunderbolt." I raised one paw inquiringly. "Why? Maybe it was just a joke."

I looked at Mr. John.

"Well," he said, "I guess he didn't want to leave us his story. Strictly speaking, he owns the copyright."

"Copyright?" said Sebastian.

"An author's right to decide what happens to his story." Mr. John sighed. "I only hope he hasn't subjected my computer at home to such drastic treatment."

I only had the beginning of the story in the computer back home, but . . . It was then I grasped the truth:

"THE LORD OF THE FERRETS" HAD FINALLY DEPARTED.

✳ ✳ ✳

The cut on my head turned out to be less serious than it had looked at first. Mr. John attributed my headache to a hamster's immune system, which vigorously reacts to even a minor trauma. After all, we hamsters are hypersensitive creatures.

Bertha had nonetheless insisted on smearing the cut with ointment. I wouldn't have objected to this if she hadn't warned me not to lick it off under any circumstances — *me*, a civilized golden hamster who would soon be writing another bestseller!

I had then retired to my nest for some shut-eye in accordance with Great-Grandmother's motto: "If you ever get sick, twelve hours' sleep will do the trick." Sure enough, when I crawled out of my nest almost exactly twelve hours later, my headache had completely disappeared.

On the other hand, Enrico and Caruso were standing outside my cage.

"To judge by that face he's pulling," said Enrico, "the sight of us gives him a headache."

"But why should it?" Caruso objected.

"Because, of course," said Enrico, "he's wondering what we have in store for him."

"Cheer up, Freddy," said Caruso, "it's nothing bad. Would it interest you to know why we're here?"

Intensely. As intensely as whether the man in the moon suffers from fleas. I yawned and proceeded to give my fur a thorough grooming.

The guinea pigs exchanged a glance. "The thing is," said Caruso, "we wanted to recite our latest poem to you."

"We'd appreciate your opinion on it," said Enrico. "I mean, since you're such an acknowledged expert on poetry."

So that, at least, had sunk into their thick skulls. I discontinued my toilette.

"It's a self-critical poem," said Caruso, looking a trifle sheepish.

REALLY? I couldn't wait to hear it. What did those conceited guinea pigs regard as self-critical?

"It's called 'The Aged Hamster's Lament.'"

What? "Just a minute, you guys." I sat up on my haunches. "Heaven help you if this is another of your —"

But they'd already started to declaim their poem in unison:

"The aged hamster shed a tear
on looking back at his career.
He'd learned to read and write, it's true,
and even had books published too.
For writing he'd earned quite a name
and reveled in his youthful fame.
But that was long ago, he grieved,
and what, in fact, had he achieved?
'What's left of me?' he asked himself.
'Just dog-eared volumes on a shelf.'"

That was just about the most unforgivable attack on a book-writing hamster since book-writing hamsters existed.

I could respond to it in one of two ways: Either as a hamster, in which case Templeton Castle's first-aid kit wouldn't contain enough bandages to cover their wounds; or as an author, in which case I would ignore their shoddy little poem. Unfortunately, both those alternatives were out of the question: The first because I was a civilized domesticated animal; the second because, well, I simply couldn't bring myself to let them get away with it.

So I reared up, inflated my cheek pouches, bared my teeth, and . . .

"Freddy!" Sir William, who had been in Mr. John's room, appeared at the top of the stairs.

Okay, carry on, Your Lordship: We mustn't be unfair . . .

"We mustn't be unfair, must we?" He

came down the stairs. "Besides, old boy, it would have been a wonderful opportunity for you to practice."

"PRACTICE? PRACTICE WHAT?"

"The thing you hamsters obviously can't do: Laugh at yourselves."

There's nothing I'd like better, Your Lordship, but I don't see the slightest reason to.

Sir William turned to Enrico and Caruso. "Your poem, gentlemen, was first-rate." The guinea pigs beamed. "Mind you," he went on, " 'dusty' might have been preferable to 'dog-eared.' "

Their smiles vanished, and they glowered at him resentfully.

Even at the expense of agreeing with Enrico and Caruso for once, I impulsively decided to punish Sir William for his unwarranted intrusion into my own literary domain.

"I beg to differ," I told him sniffily. " 'Just dusty' would have sounded most inelegant. 'Dog-eared' is absolutely fine."

CHAPTER TWENTY-FOUR

ENRICO AND CARUSO'S grand farewell show in the rabbit warren took place the following day.

Why so soon? Because Mr. John had spoken with Linda on the phone.

His real purpose in calling her had been to inquire whether his computer was still intact — unlike her laptop. Linda, who was looking after the apartment in our absence, assured him that it was. (My famously hypersensitive ears picked this up with ease because Mr. John had turned up the volume on his cell phone pretty high.) I tactfully refrained from listening to the longish conversation that followed.

Suddenly, however, came a pause. Mr. John said nothing and neither did Linda. Then I heard, "Please come home, John. I miss you."

Hmm. The volume of verse I'm planning to publish

(that's right, the one titled *A Hamster in Love*) includes a poem called "Missing Sophie." But *was* I missing Sophie, my mistress before I moved in with Mr. John? Was I really missing her unique scent of sunflower seeds? To be honest, I hadn't thought of her once throughout our time at Templeton Castle, nor had I recorded on the laptop the poem I'd composed for her during our flight to England — which would have been a waste of time in any case. However, I still had it in my head.

Enrico and Caruso staged their farewell performance under the bramble bushes behind the barn, in the open space with the rabbit hole that served as an artistes' entrance.

The whole of the rabbit colony had assembled. They greeted Sir William and me by enthusiastically drumming on the ground with their hind legs. Sir William, quite unhampered by his war wounds, bowed low. Being unprepared for this, I almost fell off his back. I trust I didn't cut too undignified a figure.

We were conducted to our box amid the bramble shoots by a cute female rabbit with a little pink nose and dainty ears.

"Thank you, my dear," said Sir William. "May I inquire your name?"

Heavens alive, what a geriatric come-on!

The young doe bared her gleaming white teeth in a smile. "They call me Bunnykins," she simpered.

"**BUNNYKiNS!**" Sir William cried ecstatically. "What a delightful name! Well worthy of its owner," he added.

Dear oh dear, this was getting downright embarrassing. Fortunately, the pretty creature had to go. "I'm onstage in a minute," she explained.

This prompted Sir William to bombard her with good wishes for her forthcoming performance, but then it was over.

Silence fell: Marmaduke had emerged from the artistes' entrance. "Honored guests, esteemed bucks and does!" he cried. "Welcome to our grand farewell show! Since our program is a lengthy one, let us begin right away! Here they are once more, the universally popular double act . . . Enrico and Caruso!"

The guinea pigs duly appeared.

As before, when they made their entrance, the ground shook and the air vibrated as fifty rabbits drummed their hind legs.

Enrico and Caruso spent a while bowing in all directions, and the deafening thumping persisted. Finally, they raised their forepaws for silence.

"Thank you, friends!" said Caruso, pretending to speak into a microphone. Thanks to Interanimal, our telepathic language, he contrived to make his voice resound so loudly in our heads that one might have been forgiven for thinking the two of them had installed an amplifier of at least 10,000 watts.

"First, friends," said Enrico, also into an imaginary mike, "let us express our heartfelt gratitude" — he and Caruso pointed in our direction — "TO OUR TWO HEROE IN THE BATTLE WITH THE FERRETS!"

The drumming that followed was quite as deafening as before. Sir William rose and bowed. So did I, cutting a more dignified figure this time.

When we resumed our seats, Sir William looked at me in silence.

"All right," I conceded, "that was very gracious of them."

"And now," Caruso said into his mike, "we're going to start with the song we promised you, but which we never got to sing for reasons known to you all — the song we composed specially for you, and —"

"Make it snappy, Caruso," Enrico cut in, "or there'll be another nasty interruption."

The rabbits laughed.

Caruso called something to the artistes' entrance, and out tripped three young does led by Bunnykins. Having taken up their positions, they started to hum and sway.

They were obviously the backup group.

"So here it is," said Enrico. "Our 'Hymn to the Brave.'"

Standing side by side — scrawny Enrico with his long red-and-white fur, and corpulent Caruso in his short coat of black and white — they proceeded to sing.

Their performance was a hundred percent professional, I have to admit, and the young does' rendering of the refrain was a feast for the ear.

"Whatever kind of bird or beast
we are, what truly matters least
is our appearance. We belong
together. So join in our song:
Fur coats or feathers, big or small,
we are God's creatures one and all."

The trio of female rabbits lingered soulfully on the last syllable.

"We may like cows in pastures graze
or spend our time in other ways,
like chasing after mice and voles,
or breed like rabbits in their holes.
Whether we squeak or mew or neigh,
we are God's creatures come what may."

At this point, unfortunately, the backing trio was drowned out by a fiftyfold roar of laughter from the rabbits, many of whom repeated the lines preceding the chorus to one another. Sir William gave me a sidelong glance. "You see?" it said. "*They* can laugh at themselves."

Enrico and Caruso were now holding the imaginary mikes close to their mouths. They managed to make their voices sound not only louder but nearer, as if their song were addressed to each of us individually:

"The most important thing by far
is whether we courageous are,
and whether we our fears withstand
like Freddy and his feline friend.
No matter if we're big or small,
we are God's creatures one and all."

They repeated the last two lines several times, backed by the female rabbits. Then, before the audience could start applauding, Caruso called out, "We dedicate that song to all courageous tomcats, book-writing hamsters, and — last but not least — all brave thumpers in the world!"

Did I once say I knew what a wild ovation was? Well, *now* I knew. The rabbits drummed so hard, I feared for my eardrums.

Sir William didn't drum, of course. He clapped sedately, using his forepaws, but he did call, "**BRavo! BRavissimo!**"— which was pretty wild by his standards.

I clapped likewise, to convey that I was equally enthusiastic. Which, to be quite honest, I genuinely was.

And then we bade the rabbits farewell.

Before we did, however, we had to sit through a lot more high jinks onstage (as Great-Grandmother would have put it). Some of the acts weren't bad, but none of them could hold a candle to "Hymn to the Brave."

Lucinda, Nibbles, and Marmaduke came to our box after the show. Enrico and Caruso weren't present. They would be saying their good-byes at a big farewell party in the rabbit warren.

"You're cordially invited too, of course," Lucinda told us. "The only thing is, it's a rabbit-and-guinea-pig party."

"Meaning what?" I asked.

IT'S a CELERY PARTY!" she said, her eyes shining. "There'll be nothing but celery to eat."

"Many thanks, my dear," Sir William said hurriedly, "but I think it's time I rejoined Mr. John."

"Fr . . . Fr . . ." Nibbles performed a gigantic leap in my direction. "Freddy! How about you?!"

A hamster in the midst of fifty rabbits and two guinea pigs, all munching celery? "Er, thank you," I said, "but I still have a poem to finish."

Nibbles gave me an understanding nod. "Ah, ye . . . yes, you writers," he said, gazing meditatively into space. "Always intent on higher things."

"Tell me, my dear sir," said Marmaduke, "will you be publishing a book about your experiences here?"

I nodded. "Probably."

He drew himself up. "In that case, being the principal character, I insist on your reading it aloud to me first, so that I can check its accuracy."

"Well, er . . ." I looked up at him, quite speechless.

His expression was condescending in the extreme.

Then a fit of fury overcame me. Who did he think he was?! My books were never read aloud for anyone to check, least of all a bumptious rabbit!

I reared up on my haunches.

Just then I happened to catch sight of Sir William. He was sitting there sedately with his tail curled around him, watching us.

And suddenly I saw the scene through his eyes: A supercilious rabbit so stupid that even a refined tomcat could only describe him as a nitwit, and confronting him, with fur bristling and teeth bared, a furious little golden hamster on the verge of causing mayhem.

I pictured this scene in every detail.

And couldn't help laughing so hard that I almost fell over backward.

❋　❋　❋

Although our departure was only hours away, Sebastian had kindly set up his computer in our tower room.

"Would you do me a favor?" I asked Sir William. "Would you go and get Annabelle for me — preferably without making any snide . . ." But he'd already given me an arch wink. He left the room, smirking to himself. What lingered with me, although he hadn't uttered it again, was a vivid memory of his earlier remark: "Not thinking of cheating on little Sophie, are you?"

I should like to make this absolutely clear: Sophie will always be Sophie, my first mistress, who smells so deliciously of sunflower seeds!

But there's also such a scent as chamomile blossom.

Heaven knows I'm not one of those fickle hamsters whose motto is "The grass is always greener," but I only had the poem in my head and might easily forget it if I didn't get it down on a computer before long. After all, it's a writer's duty to preserve his works for posterity. . . .

Then Annabelle came in.

"Hi, Freddy," she said. She sat down at the table, enveloping me in her divine scent of chamomile blossom.

"So you're off soon," she went on. "It's a shame." She looked at me sadly. "A great shame." Fiercely, she added, "In fact, it's a *crying* shame!"

Annabelle, I wrote on the screen, *I want to give you something. As a souvenir.*

"a souvenir? of you, you mean?"

I nodded. And then, while she watched, I wrote:

TO ANNABELLE
The very thought of you, my dear,
is one I cherish very much.
My eyes light up when you are near,
my whiskers quiver at your touch.
Cheek pouches swelling with delight,
I fill my nostrils with your scent.
Whene'er my eyes on you alight,
no hamster could feel more content.

✳ ✳ ✳

We were back home in our apartment.

Sir William, having devoured a big helping of canned sardines immediately on arrival, had stretched out on his blanket with a pleasurable sigh. Enrico and Caruso were sitting in front of the TV, able at last to continue their artistic training — or so they claimed.

Mr. John had turned on his computer. "I know it's an old chestnut," he said, "but it's true for all that: East or west, home is best."

Even so, I couldn't help thinking — rather wistfully — of our final farewell to Templeton Castle. . . .

We had been about to board our taxi, with the meter already ticking in the courtyard.

"When I think of all that's happened since you got here!" Lord Templeton said, shaking his head, "— all that really *shouldn't* have happened."

Mr. John grinned. "Things have a habit of happening by themselves."

"There's something else that really shouldn't happen," said Bertha, pointing to me. "The fact that such a little creature writes such great big books. It's abnormal. You can't convince me it's good for him."

"What about guinea pigs that make up poems?" said Sebastian.

"That's abnormal too," Bertha said gruffly. "And they didn't pee on the floor once. **THAT'S EVEN MORE ABNORMAL.**"

"Freddy," said Sebastian, "write a cool story about what happened here. Be sure to make it really exciting, won't you?"

I nodded.

Annabelle came over to me. "Thank you for the souvenir, Freddy," she said softly. "I've printed it out and framed it."

And then our taxi drove off.

DIETLOF REICHE grew up in a family of five children. Over the years, the family adopted seven hamsters, but unfortunately, they eventually all ran away. Dietlof always wondered why they left and where they went. So he imagined Freddy, and there began the Golden Hamster Saga. Dietlof Reiche lives in Hamburg, Germany, with his wife.

JOHN BROWNJOHN has garnered many awards for his translations of more than one hundred books for children and adults, including the Helen and Kurt Wolff Prize, the U.S. PEN Prize, and the Christopher Award. He lives in Dorset, England.

JOE CEPEDA has created artwork for numerous book covers, magazines, and newspapers. He is also the illustrator of many award-winning picture books. He lives in California with his family.

BE SURE TO READ ALL OF FREDDY'S ADVENTURES!

I, FREDDY
BOOK ONE IN THE GOLDEN HAMSTER SAGA

FREDDY IN PERIL
BOOK TWO IN THE GOLDEN HAMSTER SAGA

FREDDY TO THE RESCUE
BOOK THREE IN THE GOLDEN HAMSTER SAGA

COMING SOON . . .

FREDDY'S FINAL QUEST
BOOK FIVE IN THE GOLDEN HAMSTER SAGA